"Lieutenant War[...] [...]s you guys find," Ron s[...] [...]1 we got here. Said y[...] [...]e situation out there."

Adams leaned back, frowned, and rubbed his forehead. "It's one of the worst disasters I've ever seen. We got about four inches of rain the first hour. Since everything burned in the Thomas Fire, the ground couldn't absorb it. There's two hundred fifty-nine thousand acres of nothing but ashes up there in the mountains. All the dirt got washed downhill, creating tidal waves of mud in the mountain canyons. The waves followed the creek beds downstream into the flat land in Montecito, where they spread out and bulldozed everything in their path. The flow continued right on down Olive Mill Road and onto the freeway. Mud is twenty feet deep down there."

He gazed intently at the detectives. "I've got teams out searching for bodies with cadaver dogs. When they find one, the crew will call you. They'll send someone to guide you in. It's your show from there. Notify the coroner when it's time to remove the body. Be real careful where you walk. One wrong step and you can disappear."

Ticket to Paradise

by

Michael Preston

Ticket to Paradise

Cover Art by *Lisa Dawn MacDonald*

The Wild Rose Press, Inc.
PO Box 708
Adams Basin, NY 14410-0708
Visit us at www.thewildrosepress.com

Publishing History
First Edition, 2022
Trade Paperback ISBN 978-1-5092-4369-3
Digital ISBN 978-1-5092-4370-9

Published in the United States of America

Dedication

To my wife Pat, who always encouraged me to press
on, even in the dark days.

Acknowledgments

It was easy to write the first draft of this novel, but that was merely the beginning of the journey. It needed editing, over and over, until it reached the state where it could be published. I wish to thank Kristina Stanley for some early editing advice which opened my eyes that my book was way too long. Cutting it down was painful but necessary. Kaycee John was my second editor, who never gave up on me through the countless revisions which followed. Without her editing skill and continuous encouragement that it was almost there, I would not be here today.

Thanks also to my family members, Manuel, John, Steve, and others who provided encouragement and advice when I was wandering in the wilderness. You guys are the best.

Prologue

January 8th

At three a.m. the nondescript stucco house at the top of a gently rising slope stood silent. In the deep purple darkness that surrounded the Santa Inez Mountains above Montecito, California, rain poured in relentless sheets, drumming loudly on the roof, drowning all it touched. Violent torrents of water threatened to overflow the banks of the rocky creek that flowed through the backyard. In the distance, a growl of thunder announced nature's mastery of the land.

Inside the house, a lone woman bore witness to the event. She sat, unmoving, in an easy chair near the living room window that looked out onto the back yard, a dark shape in the unlit house, indifferent to the fury raging outside.

A faint rumbling disturbed the rain, growing louder as time slipped by. The ground vibrated, rattling the dishes in the kitchen cupboard. Still, she did not move. Within seconds, the origin of the rumbling became clear: a monstrous wave of mud, boulders, and debris rushed toward the house.

As it crashed through the rear windows, the giant mass overwhelmed everything in its path. Water pressed against the front windows, rapidly flooding the house. The pressure grew until shards of glass blew out like missiles into the yard. Carried along on the raging tempest, the woman slid through the ruined bay window, riding the wave until her body tumbled end over end, sucked down into the mud.

Chapter One

Wading knee deep through mud on a chilly January morning, Detective Ron Jackson struggled to reach his destination: a large pine tree standing alone in the middle of the devastation left by a massive mud slide. A body, impaled on a broken branch, dangled ten feet off the ground. The rank odor of decaying flesh forced the need to wear a bandana over his face to keep from gagging.

He studied the corpse. A young male, age estimated at around fifteen, dressed in jeans and a light jacket. To be that high in the tree, a giant wave of mud must have slammed him into it. Ron hoped the kid died before that happened.

Until the body was retrieved from the tree, there was nothing more to do. That unpleasant duty was the job of the coroner. With a heavy sigh, he made the call, advising them to bring a ladder. It would be two hours before anyone arrived.

This was the third body found in a tree. Every day brought more death and decomposed remains; by now he felt numb to it all. Identifying missing people had been his sole job since early December—and he couldn't remember a day going by in the last month when he'd not had to deal with the dead. If this continued much longer, he feared serious psychological damage to his psyche. He was a detective, charged with investigating crimes against persons, not identifying endless numbers of dead people. But no one cared about his opinion. Two freakish back-to-back natural disasters, which no one could have foreseen, had led to his sorry state.

It started with the Thomas Fire that raged for almost the entire month of December. Two hundred thousand acres of parched land burned, leaving the mountains above Montecito, California denuded of vegetation.

The Santa Barbara County Sheriff's Office, shorthanded as always, threw Ron into the fray. Countless hours were spent pouring over lists, compiled by Red Cross staffers, of people staying at evacuation centers, then matching them to the names of those reported missing—and trying to determine who was still alive and who was dead. He worked through Christmas, the peak day of the fire, finally getting a few days off in January. After dragging his weary body home, and wishing himself a happy new year, he slept for two days. Upon returning to work, a month's worth of neglected paperwork sat on his desk. He hated paperwork.

The second disaster struck on January eighth. Ron was back on his regular shift, looking forward to a weekend off at his home in Carpinteria. His boss, Lieutenant Warner, put a quick end to that.

"Get your ass up here ASAP. The County declared another emergency. Thanks to the rain, we've got mud and bodies everywhere down in Montecito. The 101 is buried under a ton of mud, so driving is not an option. See if the train is running. If not, figure something out. Plan on staying in town until the freeway gets cleared; you're authorized to use the county per diem for a room."

Ron kept his groan to himself. He'd rather work traffic duty than do missing persons again. After packing a bag with a few days' worth of fresh clothes, he waved goodbye to his comfortable bed and took off to the train station, where more bad news awaited.

"I need a ticket to Santa Barbara," he told the person at the Amtrak ticket window.

The clerk gave a bark of laughter. "You and everybody else, pal. Didn't you see the news? The tracks got buried in the mudslides that went through Montecito. Be days before we can dig them out."

That left him with, as the lieutenant put it, "figuring something out."

After a few desperate calls, he discovered the airport was also shut down. The only form of transportation to Santa Barbara was a ferry boat out of Ventura, fifty miles farther South. This was the worst possible news. He got seasick just looking at boats. But unless he wanted to hike to work, there were no other options.

The normal commute by car to the Santa Barbara Sheriff's Office where he was assigned, usually took only thirty minutes. By boat, it took hours. Once the ferry left the confines of the Ventura harbor, the sea grew choppy from the remains of the storm. While standing anchored near the stern of the ferry, he chanted, *I'm going to be okay,* and tried to think happy thoughts.

It didn't work.

Thirty minutes later, he fed the fish his breakfast, and remained seasick for the rest of the trip.

Arriving late that afternoon, he staggered off the boat, grateful to be on solid ground, despite the vicious stomach cramps which didn't seem to abate. *Never again will I set foot on a boat.*

It didn't get any better. The Twilight Inn, a motel once fashionable in 1959, sported a mattress that had more lumps than a field of gopher holes. Sleeping on a rock would have been more comfortable. A pillow, beaten into submission years ago, provided no support for his head. Towels in the bath were thin enough to see through. It was the only place available for the miserly per diem the County paid for travel. Sleeping on the ground in a tent would have been an upgrade.

He dutifully called the LT to report his arrival in town. "I've arrived on scene, Loo."

"Jackson! It's four o'clock. What—you decided to walk?"

Ron explained how a ferry turned out to be the only means of transport, omitting the part about getting seasick. Nobody needed to hear that.

As usual, the LT only half listened to his complaints. Ron heard the gears turning inside the guy's head as he put together a mental task list.

"Okay, okay. Not your fault," he said, when Ron finished. "Look, it's a cluster fuck out there. Half of Montecito is buried in mud. I went out to see for myself this morning and I've never seen anything this bad. The number of missing persons is rising by the minute. I've got a bad feeling we're going to have more dead than from the Thomas fire, so I need you and Mary Ann to get over there and work with the search and rescue crew."

"She's back?" Ron said, surprised and not a little delighted.

Mary Ann McDonald, his longtime partner, had been on maternity leave since November. He hadn't expected her back for a few more weeks.

"When she heard there might be a lot of dead people to investigate, she couldn't stand it any longer. Came in this morning and reported for duty. Been out in the field all day," Warner said. "Call her. She can pick you up tomorrow morning. There's a command post you'll be working out of until the freeway gets cleaned up. It shouldn't be more than a couple of days. You'll be coordinating with Sergeant Adams; head of the search and rescue teams. Questions?"

"No, sir."

"Okay, keep me apprised."

Chapter Two

January 9th

"I thought they condemned this place," Mary Ann McDonald wisecracked.

A few years younger than Ron, her turquoise eyes sparkled mischievously under a mop of strawberry blonde hair. After she was promoted to detective a few years back, the LT had assigned Ron to be her training officer. He found her to be ambitious and a hard worker. They worked well together and had stayed partners after her training was completed.

Since she lived in Santa Barbara, her commute to work was unaffected by the mudslides that occurred south of the city. In a call the day before, Ron gave her the address of the motel and made plans for her to pick him up.

The clock in a church bell tower down the street struck six, disturbing the quiet morning as he eased into her car. "They reopened it just for me," he said. "I got the penthouse. It comes with an extra towel." He studied his partner. "I didn't expect to see you for another couple of weeks. Heard you begged the LT to come back early. He said you refused to be away from me any longer."

She snorted. "No, you heard it wrong. He begged *me* to come back. Said you fucked up the cases so badly the chief threatened to fire you."

"Are you kidding? The chief loves me. So what happened? Cabin fever or crying baby syndrome?"

Before taking leave, she told him about an affair with a man named Manuel that ended with her getting pregnant. Divorced with two kids from his previous marriage, he did not want to start over, so she had full custody of the baby. Ron suspected Manuel was enlisted as a sperm donor, so she could have a kid before her biological clock ticked down. Besides, she was far too driven to succeed in her career to want a husband.

He wondered if she had lost all the baby fat. A fitness fanatic, Mary Ann kept in good shape before the pregnancy, doing aerobics five times a week at the gym. She had complained constantly during the pregnancy about how fat she was getting. Today a brown jump suit smudged with mud obscured her figure.

"Tomas is all right. He sleeps most of the night. I can't pry him away from Mom. I just missed the action. Since this is the biggest thing that's ever happened around here, I didn't want to listen to *your* war stories for the rest of my life."

This was only partially true. The high command handpicked her to be fast-tracked into a management spot after it was pointed out that no women existed on the force above the rank of sergeant. She made detective in five years, leapfrogging over more senior males, and making some enemies.

Against his wishes, Ron had been assigned to be her training officer. His belief was that someone being fast tracked would have a sense of entitlement, making them lazy and difficult to train. But after a rocky start, Mary Ann earned his respect by working hard, and never asking for favors. The disaster was an opportunity to burnish her credentials, to show she deserved her rank. She couldn't do that on maternity leave.

He smiled. "Cabin fever it is. Glad you're back, the paperwork is piling up. That damn Thomas Fire put me back a month. I'll find you a desk somewhere so you can catch up on it while I'm out detecting."

She slugged him on the arm. "Bite me, Jackson. I've got to make sure your sorry ass doesn't fall into a sinkhole somewhere. Nobody else around here would even notice you were missing."

"Not true. My mother calls me every month."

She rolled her eyes. "How'd you get up here?"

Ron explained again about the ferry, again omitting the part about getting seasick.

"So, how was the trip into town, sailor boy?" She grinned, as if finding a particular memory rather funny. "Remember that time we had to go to Catalina on the ferry and you puked all the way there and back?"

He'd forgotten about the Catalina trip, having sworn he would never get on a boat again for the rest of his life. It cost him a very expensive dinner to buy Mary Ann's silence then. This time, she would likely demand a new car. Otherwise it would be leaked to everyone in homicide how the great Detective Ron Jackson couldn't look at a boat without puking his brains out. The story would be embellished with each telling until he wouldn't be able to show his face at any police station in town.

Frowning, he pretended not to hear. "What happened out in the field yesterday?"

"Oh no, not again!" she shrieked, not about to let this go. "Did you puke all over your clothes? You're not riding in my car if you smell like something that got run over on the freeway a week ago."

He sighed and mustered as much dignity as he could find. "There is nothing wrong with me. If you start any rumors to the contrary, I will shoot you myself. Not to mention you will lose your only friend. Now, are you going to shut up and drive?"

She was still chuckling as she made the right turn into the command post parking lot. Cops swarmed the area, coming and going from all directions, along with civilians assigned to the rescue effort. The sound of heavy machinery mixed with the shouts of orders from the crew supervisors.

The detectives entered a narrow, single-wide trailer, which served as headquarters for the rescue operation. A passage toward the back of the trailer wound between desks jammed together. Phones rang intermittently. Topographical maps hung on the walls. A clerk sitting at a desk barred their way.

"We're looking for Adams," said Ron. The clerk nodded, jerking a thumb over his shoulder without bothering to check their ID's.

Near the back, a man sat behind a messy steel desk, talking on his landline. The detectives threaded their way around the other desks to get there. Adams glanced up as they flashed their shields. Waving them to a couple of worn chairs, he finished the phone conversation and stood to shake hands. "Pete Adams, Search and Rescue."

Coarse salt and pepper hair perched over a face lined with wrinkles from too much sun after twenty-three years as a cop. A pair of black-rimmed glasses gave him a professorial vibe. A strong square jaw, just like Dick Tracy's, completed his looks. He gazed unblinking at the detectives. "What can I do for you guys?"

"Lieutenant Warner assigned us to ID any bodies

you guys find," Ron said. "He told me to find you when we got here. Said you might have some intel on the situation out there."

Adams leaned back, frowned, and rubbed his forehead. "It's one of the worst disasters I've ever seen. We got about four inches of rain the first hour and it didn't stop. Since everything burned in the Thomas Fire, the ground couldn't absorb it. There's two hundred fifty-nine thousand acres of nothing but ashes up there in the mountains. All the dirt got washed downhill, creating tidal waves of mud in the mountain canyons. The waves followed the creek beds downstream into the flat land in Montecito, where they spread out and bulldozed everything in their path. The flow continued right on down Olive Mill Road and onto the freeway. The mud is probably twenty feet deep down there."

He paused to take a drink from the water bottle on his desk. "We're compiling a list of reported missing persons and trying to check their houses first, but it's tough as hell. Some of the buildings just aren't there anymore, got picked up by the mud and carried on downstream. The street numbers on the curbs are under the mud, so unless we locate a number on the house itself, we have to guess."

"Jeez," Mary Ann muttered. "Gotta be tough."

"Tell me about it," Adams said. "I've got teams out searching for bodies with cadaver dogs. When they find one, the crew will call you and send someone to guide you in. It's your show from there. Notify the coroner when it's time to remove the body. Be real careful where you walk. One wrong step and you can disappear."

Ron sensed this was an assignment way worse than the Thomas Fire. Visions of climbing over mountains of mud stuck in his brain. This was work for the young bucks, not him.

When he was younger, working out every week to keep in shape had been important. It fed the illusion he was still a stud. But as each year passed, it took more work to keep pace. Eventually, he tired of the battle and gave up, letting his gym membership lapse.

Now Rogaine was the key in a battle to keep what hair he had left from disappearing. His intense blue eyes still intimidated suspects, but he needed glasses to see the fine print on a page. Under a rather ordinary nose, a bushy mustache contained a few more gray hairs every year, which reminded him of encroaching old age every time he looked in a mirror. Even though he was only forty-two, and way too young to feel old, bouts of depression attacked him. Mary Ann told him it was a classic mid-life crisis.

Ron figured God was out to get him.

He sat stewing over his mud monkey fate. With nothing to be done, Ron gave a heavy sigh and looked up. "Can we get a copy of the missing persons list?"

"Of course. I update it every evening based upon feedback from my teams and you guys. I'll have a new one ready at 0700 every day. We have a quick meeting here to compare notes before heading out to the field. As long as there is any possibility of someone being alive out there, we work until it gets dark."

Pete handed over the list. Three pages long; single spaced, and containing the name, address, and phone number, if known, of the missing person, and any distinguishing marks on their body. It also contained information on the person who reported them missing.

After the detectives requisitioned a couple of desks

in the trailer, Ron scanned the pages. "It's going to take us months to chase down all these names."

"Most of them are probably fine, and living off the grid," Mary Ann offered. "It never occurs to them to contact anybody."

"Maybe they don't want their family to know where they are."

Mary Ann chuckled.

It took only half an hour for the phone to ring.

Chapter Three

"Team Leader Jim Dawson here. We found a body, adult female, about three quarters of a mile up Olive Mill Road. One of my team will guide you up."

"Roger that," Ron said." Give me the coordinates.""

The detectives drove to the meet point, where Brad Kaminski, a member of the team, waited. With hip boots and a jumpsuit caked in mud, a face smeared dark brown, and a hard hat more brown than white, he looked like he'd just finished mud wrestling with a pig.

By now, everything buried in the mud had decayed, creating a smell somewhat like sour milk. The odor caught in their throats as the detectives exited their car.

After introductions all around, Kaminski grinned. "Okay guys, get suited up. We've got to hike in about a mile before we get to the body,"

"A mile?" Ron said, giving the surrounding devastation a jaundiced look.

"All the roads are full of mud. It's impossible to get any vehicles in there," Kaminski said. "It doesn't get real deep until just before we get there."

Unsure he could survive a hike through the knee-deep mud without needing CPR, Ron gave Mary Ann a questioning look. She shrugged and turned to get her gear out of the trunk.

They were led through some of the most devastated terrain they had ever seen. Destroyed buildings and splintered remains of trees littered the area. It looked like a war zone. Mud made a sucking noise around their boots as they tried to take a step. It was eerily quiet; even the birds had taken off for better territory.

They plowed ahead, staying close to their guide. As the mud got deeper, their pace slowed. Brad probed the muck ahead of him with a long stick, searching for sinkholes. By the time they arrived, each of them were panting hard. The search team stood by impassively, trained not to disturb any evidence until the detectives inspected the scene.

Their destination was a small grove of pepper trees that somehow had withstood the tidal wave of destruction. The remains of a ruined house stood a short distance uphill. Deep in the grove, team members stared into a hole dug out of the mud.

"What have you got?" Ron asked, struggling to catch his breath without the others seeing how out of shape he was.

Jim Dawson said, "Looks like a female, late thirties or early forties. Probably got washed out of that house up there." He waved toward the ruined house maybe seventy feet uphill.

About two feet down in the hole they saw the upper torso of the victim. Her face angled up at them, eyes closed, hair stuck to her head by clumps of mud. Possibly Caucasian, but all the mud caked on her made identifying her race impossible at the scene.

"Who found her?" Mary Ann asked.

"The cadaver dogs kept ranging over to this spot, so we started digging."

"You find anything else?" Ron asked, knowing artifacts found with the body sometimes helped with identification

Dawson shook his head. "Nothing so far."

"Did you check out the house yet?"

"We didn't have time before we found the body."

Ron arched a brow at his partner, who shrugged. Another routine accidental death, nothing more to do right now. "Okay, you can dig her out. We're going to check the house, then we'll be back."

They waded back to the street and followed it to the ruined house, probing their way through the mud with poles they borrowed from the team, until they arrived at the front door. Ron's legs felt like lead. He glanced enviously at Mary Ann, who looked like she could do another mile without breaking a sweat.

Torn off its foundation, the house listed to the right. The stucco was spider-webbed with large cracks that ran up to the roof. None of the windows contained glass. Ron pointed to the area below where a porch light dangled by one wire. Numbers were tacked to the house there, covered in mud. Mary Ann wiped away the mud and wrote the numbers down in her notebook. He shined his flashlight through the blown out front window. There was nothing to see except a sea of mud.

"I'll go right," he said. "You go left."

With a nod, she waded off to the left and around the house. Ron proceeded around the right side, shining his light into every window he found. There was nothing of interest. By the time he reached the backyard, the mud touched the roof, blocking the windows. His partner appeared at the opposite corner and shook her head. He pointed back the way she came, and they met near the front door. At this point, it was still too dangerous for them to enter the house.

"The mud hit it from the rear and just carried it off its foundation," Ron said.

"Must have been horrendous. That girl never had a chance."

"If she was in the house," he said.

"True. We'll find out soon enough; we've got the house number."

They returned to the grove of trees where the body of the dead woman now lay on top of the ground. Despite the caked mud, they saw she wore jeans and a blouse. No shoes, but the mud might have sucked them off her feet.

"You want to do the search?"

Mary Ann nodded, kneeled down next to the body, and searched for ID. "Nothing in her pockets," she murmured. "No jewelry either."

As Ron took more pictures, he said, "Call the coroner."

****

Back at the command post, they hosed the mud off their boots and settled down at their desks. Ron retrieved the missing persons report out of a drawer and squinted at it.

"When will you quit pretending you don't need glasses?" Mary Ann said.

He took a pair of reading glasses out of his shirt pocket. "I can see fine without these, but I'll wear them to make you happy," he said, trying for dignity.

"You're getting old, partner. Denial just makes it worse."

He mumbled something unintelligible and scanned the list, searching for a number to match the one on the destroyed house. There were no matches. "Shit."

Without a match they hoped for, quick identification

wasn't possible. He would have to wait until the coroner washed off all the mud before taking a picture of her face, then show it to everyone who'd reported a missing woman about the same age to see if anyone could ID her.

Once identified, the detectives would strike one more name off their missing persons list. Another routine investigation closed.

Or so he thought.

Chapter Four

January 12th

By late afternoon, Ron hadn't gotten any more calls from the search and rescue guys. That alone was cause for celebration. Nobody wanted to go outside. A light but steady rain that started early that morning had turned the dirt parking lot at the command post into a sea of mud. To make it worse, a wind kicked up, strong enough to rattle the windows and rock the trailer.

When the phone rang, he groaned, fearing a call-out would ruin his day. Instead, Alonzo Velasquez, the County Coroner, wanted to talk. "I found something interesting about the Jane Doe you dug out of the mud. Once we got her cleaned up, I noticed it right away."

"Do tell."

"She was dead before the mudslide buried her."

Surprised, Ron sat up a little straighter. "How do you know?"

"Shot, right below the heart, close range. No signs of asphyxiation or blunt force trauma," Alonzo said. "You've got a murder investigation with this one, pal."

His mind began to race. "Any chance it might be suicide? Do you have a time of death?"

"Too soon to tell. An autopsy will determine that. It will take a day or two."

"Any other wounds on the body?"

"Scratches and bruises around her neck. Possibly the result of being tossed around in the mudslide."

"Call me when you have something." Ron hung up, then stared out the window, crossed his arms, and thought about what to do next.

"What?" said Mary Ann, who had been listening to his side of the phone call from her adjoining desk.

He repeated what Alonzo told him.

"Dead *before* the mudslide? No way!" she said. "But with the mud on her, we couldn't have seen a bullet hole, and she had already bled out…"

Ron nodded. "Partner, we might be back in the detecting business. I'll call the LT, give him a heads-up, maybe talk us off mud patrol. It's going to be a relief to get back to doing what they're paying us for."

****

On speaker phone, Warner warned them to stop yanking his chain—until Mary Ann yelled back that it was true, no chain yanking involved.

"Fucking unbelievable!" he swore. "Somebody kills this woman, then a mudslide destroys the crime scene? Got to be a million to one." He went silent for a minute, then asked, "How's it going on the missing persons list?"

"It's down to less than one page and nobody's called us today," said Ron, making his pitch.

"Okay, I'm going to pull you two off of that. Report back here tomorrow morning. If they find anybody else, I'll deal with it. Meanwhile, give this your full attention. It'll hit the media soon, and I want to be out in front of it. I want daily updates. Understand?"

"Yes sir," Ron replied. After hanging up, he grinned at his partner. You may kiss my ring."

"Yes sir, let's go solve this sucker!"

Chapter Five

January 13th

Ron woke up on the lumpy mattress in his dingy motel room. His back was killing him. He crawled out of bed and did a few twists to loosen up. The depression that previously weighed him down had faded. He was back in his element, doing what he loved: detecting.

With no more mud to battle, he put on the suit that had gathered dust in the closet since he'd checked into the Twilight Inn. On the morning news, the newscaster announced the freeway had reopened. Tonight, he would get to sleep in his own bed. A fine day already.

He wondered if his one and only houseplant had survived this long with no water. A succulent needed little of anything, but he had been gone a long time. It might have died of boredom.

With his suitcase by his side, he waited by the door until Mary Ann swung into the motel parking lot at seven. "Hey, guess what? The freeway's open. You can give me a ride home tonight."

"Where does it say in my job description that I have to haul your sorry ass all over the county?"

"In the section about obeying your partner in all things."

"Sounds like a marriage vow. Last I checked, we're not married."

"That's a relief. I've been a little worried, the way you've been undressing me with your eyes lately."

Mary Ann's face reddened. "Do not get me started, Detective Jackson."

He laughed, threw his suitcase into the back of her car, and walked over to the motel office to pay his bill. The manager was sorry to see him go. Ten minutes later they hit the road.

The Sheriff's headquarters building held the police department, dispatch, and the county jail. To the right of the entrance was a large conference room used for roll call and breaks. Straight ahead, a cop sat behind a counter, answering the phones and screening visitors. Behind him, a short corridor led to a locked door.

Past the door on the right, Dispatch occupied a soundproof room. In back of that was the jail behind a locked steel door. The lieutenant had his office on the left side of the hall, followed by several other offices for administrative personnel. Three interrogation rooms, stacked on both sides of the hall, completed the front half of the building. Beyond that was a large bullpen, divided up into sections by partitions.

Six detectives occupied a choice section of the open area behind the interrogation rooms. It was considered *choice* because of an unwritten rule—whoever had to walk the fewest steps to the coffee machine had the most status. The detectives had all counted the steps, and only the LT had a shorter distance to travel.

Ron and Mary Ann occupied adjoining desks next to a coveted window whose view comprised a narrow strip of grass and a lone sickly-looking tree that never seemed to grow any taller.

At this point in an investigation, they always

discussed possibilities. Mary Ann spoke first. "It could have been suicide. Depression, combined with the storm, might have pushed her over the edge. We'll have the coroner's opinion on that soon. Or possibly a home invasion robbery gone bad, if she lived in that house up the road. That'll be difficult to prove since the mud destroyed all the crime scene evidence. We won't know if anything was stolen."

"There's also the possibility she might have been a druggie, owed somebody a bunch of cash, and wouldn't pay up," suggested Ron. "Or somebody might have held a grudge against her. Jealous wife, pissed-off lover, something like that."

An office clerk wheeling a mail cart stopped at his desk and handed him a sheet of paper. "Pete Adams faxed this over this morning. It's the latest missing persons list."

Ron scanned the list which seemed to be longer than yesterday. Not a good sign. If the list got too long, the LT might decide to put them back on mud duty. One address caught his eye.

"Mary Ann, you remember the address of that destroyed house we looked at yesterday?"

She tried to remember it, gave up, and found the address in the murder book.

"Bingo," he said. "Got a match. A guy named Art Garcia reported his sister Angela missing yesterday afternoon after Pete printed the list. She lived at that address. The description is pretty close to the body we recovered. Plus, her employer reported her as missing yesterday. She worked for the county at Child Services. They got worried when she didn't show up for work and didn't return any of their messages."

"Employees of Child Services who work with kids would have their fingerprints on file," Mary Ann said.

"Why don't you call Sacramento and ask them to send us her prints?" Ron said. "I'll call the coroner and have them get a set from the corpse. We can send both sets to forensics and see if they match. Once we're positive about who she is, it will be time to invite her brother in for a chat."

Later that morning, he emailed the two sets of prints off to forensics. In the afternoon, a match was confirmed. He emailed Alonzo the name to go with the body.

Mary Ann got to work, contacting the local wireless phone companies, tracking Angela Garcia's number to Verizon. Next, she requested a subpoena for her phone records for the last year. After that, she called a friend at Human Resources for the County.

"Nicole, this is Mary Ann."

"Hi, heard you were on maternity leave."

"Just got back. The LT needed all the help he could get with the disaster in Montecito. I need some information on a deceased person by the name of Angela Garcia who works with Child Services. I need her insurance beneficiaries, where she deposits her paycheck, the person to call in case of an emergency, and the name and phone number of her boss."

"Let me look that up."

After a couple of minutes on hold, Nicole came back on the line. "I can't give you the insurance beneficiaries because of privacy rules. Her paycheck gets deposited at the Government Employees Credit Union. The emergency contact is her brother Art Garcia, and her boss is Ricardo Rodriguez." She read off their phone numbers. "Anything more we need to do at this end?"

25

"She died on the seventh. There is an ongoing investigation into her death. No laws have been broken as far as we can tell. Keep this confidential for the time being. I'll get a subpoena for her personnel records."

Ron accessed the property records through the Recorder's Office. Angela was listed as the sole owner of the home, after inheriting it from her father when he died. This raised a question in Ron's mind. Why was Angela's brother left off the deed? Some bad blood there which might have led to murder?

A routine check with the Department of Justice confirmed Angela owned a .22 caliber semi-automatic M&P compact pistol, registered in her name. While he was in the database, he checked her brother's name and learned three weapons were registered to Art Garcia: a shotgun, a pistol, and an AR-15.

The preliminaries finished, a call needed to be made to Garcia to inform him of his sister's death. It was an unpleasant task Ron had done many times during his career, but it never got easier. He glanced at Mary Ann. "Are you ready?"

She nodded.

He picked up his phone, conferenced her on, and dialed the number.

****

Art Garcia cruised south on the 101 in his silver Camry, on his way to make a delivery, when one of his cell phones rang. He glanced at the display and saw a call from a restricted number. No information there. Since the police might be calling with information about Angela, he figured it was better to answer. "Hello?"

A male voice asked, "Is this Mr. Garcia?"

It sounded like a cop to Art. "Yeah, who's this?"

"My name is Ron Jackson. I'm a detective with the Santa Barbara County Sheriff's Office, working on the missing person report you filed on your sister. We discovered the body of a woman buried in the mudslide up by Olive Mill Road yesterday. I'm very sorry to have to tell you this, but we've confirmed through fingerprints it was your sister, Angela."

Seconds ticked by before he asked, "She's...is she dead?"

"Yes, sir. Any other immediate family members we should notify?"

"No, our parents are dead. How'd dis happen?"

"As best we can determine, a massive wave of mud struck her home during the storm. The house was knocked off its foundation and carried downstream. Your sister's body was found buried in mud in a thicket of trees. Our theory is the mud either washed her out of the house—or she got caught up in the slide when she tried to escape."

When Art made no further comment, Jackson asked, "Mr. Garcia?"

"I'm....here. Just tryin' to understand all dis. I never thought..." he paused, "that somethin' like this could happen. Where's she at now? Can I see her?"

"She is at the morgue. An autopsy is being done, standard procedure in a case like this. It'll take a few days for the results. The coroner will release the body after you verify the identity."

Art was not pleased with the delay. "An autopsy? Why? Didn't you say she died in the mudslide?"

"I did. But the coroner has to determine the official cause of death. It might be asphyxiation or trauma of some sort. An autopsy will tell us. Could I ask you a few routine questions if you don't mind? It will only take a minute."

"What?" he asked, suspicious of any questions coming from someone in law enforcement.

"Do you recall the names of Angela's friends? Some of them might have information that would help us shed some light on things. Someone she worked with, for example?"

"She never talked 'bout her friends."

"I understand. Had to ask."

Art didn't want to answer any more questions. "Listen, I'm torn up 'bout this. Could we do this some other time?"

"Sure," Ron said. "There's no rush. I'll call you when we have the autopsy results, and you can officially identify the body. We can finish this up then."

He needed a reason not to meet with the cops but saw no way out of it. "Okay. I 'preciate that."

After ending the call, he mulled over what Jackson said. The mudslide had been unforeseen, and it totally ruined his plan. Angela should have been found inside her house, in what would have looked like a robbery that went bad. Now, with no obvious motive for her murder, the police would have to consider all suspects— including him.

He wondered why Jackson had not mentioned his sister had been shot. Did they even know yet? Would they suspect him?

Panic rose in his gut. The firewall he and his sister built to protect themselves still functioned, he reminded himself. And no one had seen him at the house the night she died. *This will all die down when the cops tire of chasing dead ends.*

His plan could still work.

Despite trying to ignore them, his thoughts kept slipping back to his sister's last phone call—and the quirk of fate that wouldn't happen again in a million years.

It changed his life forever.

Chapter Six

January 7th

Curled up in her easy chair at home with her feet tucked beneath her, Angela checked the numbers on the small slip of paper for the hundredth time. The answer didn't change. A lotto ticket, bought yesterday on a whim at the local 7-Eleven, contained all of the winning numbers.

$135 million dollars. All hers.

She laughed and cried at the same time. Her entire life had been one big struggle. A crappy childhood that left permanent scars on both body and mind, followed by a five-year struggle to get that college degree, then a low-paying job at Child Services. Add to that, the constant pressure to find enough money to pay her bills, and the worry that her sideline business might land her in jail.

All that was over now. She fantasized about what it would be like to never have to work again, tell her brother to fuck off, live like a queen, and be free to do whatever she wanted.

There was one last piece of business she needed to do first. A package was ready for Art; one he'd be picking up from her tomorrow. She debated telling him the news then or calling him now. *Better to break it to him now.* Sometimes his temper could lead to bursts of anger. If that happened, it would be safer to be far away.

Dumping him would take some finesse. A good portion of his income would disappear. Maybe she'd throw a little money in the pot to soften the blow, but that was it. She didn't owe him anything.

****

Art Garcia sat in a rocker on the front porch of his ranch house in Santa Maria, listening to the tree frogs calling each other from the woods at the side of his property. A sure sign the weather was changing. Already dark clouds blocked the late afternoon sun. He had taken the day off from dealing drugs. The big payday, due to come in tomorrow, would pay the bills for a while.

A phone call from his sister ruined the moment.

"I've got something to tell you, bro. Something amazing happened to me. My life has changed; I won't need the money from our business anymore. I'm going to be straight with you. Tomorrow is it. Then I'm done."

Momentarily stunned into silence, Art put a vise grip on the phone. This had to be a joke. "What are you talkin' about? 'So long, bro, have a nice life?' Are you fuckin' with me?"

"This is no joke. It just happened today."

"What just happened today?" he mimicked, almost shouting into the phone.

"I won the lotto."

"Yeah, and I'm Batman," he replied sarcastically.

"I'm not kidding Art. I really won it."

"Jesus, how much is it worth?" he asked, calmer now as he listened to the answer. "Holy shit, Angie, we got to talk 'bout this. I'm comin' down there."

Her lame answer fueled his anger. "Bullshit, this affects me, too. I risked it all, jus' like you did. You can't just walk away and leave me with nothin'. We're

31

partners! Be there in an hour." He disconnected the call before she could reply.

He sat back in his rocker, and ran his hands through his curly black hair, trimmed close to his scalp. Large shaggy eyebrows framed angry brown eyes. At six-feet-four, he presented a menacing figure. Rippling biceps on his thirty-eight-year-old body testified to his strength. He angered quickly, but over the years had learned the hard way to keep his temper under control. But the anger he felt now seemed justified. His income was being taken away, and his sister didn't care.

****

Angela paced back and forth on the carpet in her home. She considered getting her car keys and fleeing. Unfortunately, she didn't have time to plan her escape. Where would she go? He would be here in an hour.

Instead of congratulating her, he wanted a share of the wealth. It was a stupid thing she did, telling him about it. The excitement of winning overrode common sense. She should have collected the money, quietly planned her escape and disappeared somewhere he'd never find her. The idiot would have suspected nothing. Now she faced a confrontation.

She understood the need to share the profits with Art when he'd contributed to their business. They were partners in that. But this had nothing to do with the business. The lotto money was hers alone; he'd earned none of it. Expecting her to share it was just greed. True, he would miss the money from their business, but she never promised it would last forever. Thanks to her, he had a house now, so he should show some gratitude.

She had always manipulated him into doing what she wanted; she perfected the art when they were kids.

His big sister, he always looked up to her, craving approval, and she used that to her advantage. But he had a temper, and she needed to be careful. There was a pistol in her bedroom, which she retrieved and hid in a drawer in the living room. Letting him see the gun might be enough to get him to back off if he threatened violence.

As the time ticked by, her mood matched the dark clouds forming outside. Rain would be coming soon, a front blowing in from Hawaii, sure to drench the bare ground of the Santa Ynez Mountains that loomed behind her home. People living closer to the foothills had evacuated in fear of mudslides, but no one told Angela she needed to go.

She promised herself that once through this last obstacle, she would leave California forever.

Chapter Seven

Art sped down the 101 toward Montecito, passing the off-ramp for Buellton, home to Anderson's Restaurant, famous for their pea soup.

Back in the 70s, the owner of the restaurant, whose name was Anderson, put up billboards along the major roads in California, telling travelers how much further it was to Pea Soup Andersons. A sign announced "*55 miles to Pea Soup Andersons*" with a picture of a steaming bowl of pea soup beneath it. Ten miles further along the road, another said "*45 miles to Pea Soup Andersons*", then another, and another.

Finally, a sign told the driver to "*Turn off here for Pea Soup Andersons.*"

If you were a real moron and missed it, a sign at the next exit told you to turn around, you just *passed* Pea Soup Anderson's. After forty years or more, most of the billboards had fallen down, which was fine with him. He hated peas.

He drove on, passing Isla Vista, famous for its wild parties and riots, being full of students attending the nearby University of California at Santa Barbara. From there, a short drive to Olive Mill Road. Cruising up the off ramp, he made a left to take the bridge over the freeway into Montecito, home to the stars. Several popular daytime TV hostesses and British royalty had mansions there. *And Angela Garcia.*

Just one more thing he got screwed out of. But not this time! He was getting what he deserved, and his sister would give it to him.

Heavy, rain swollen clouds blanketed the sky. Gusts of wind rocked his car. It reminded him of the huge amount of rain in the weather forecast. He vowed to get this settled with Angela quickly and get home before the storm hit.

Her home was in an older part of town, containing modest well-maintained homes on large lots. The area was gentrifying. Real estate speculators were buying anything they could get their hands on, tearing down the original homes and replacing them with mansions. He drove into the garage and closed the door. Unlike her custom, Angela was not waiting for him.

Entering the house, he slammed the door from the garage a little harder than necessary to announce his presence. He stalked down the hall, glancing into the kitchen. Not seeing anyone there, he proceeded into the living room.

She sat in an easy chair, scrutinizing him. Illuminated by the soft light from a table lamp, Art thought he detected some arrogance in her gaze. A cocktail glass on the coffee table was almost empty. A ring of water had sweated off of it.

He gave her one curt nod. "Got any beer?"

"In the frig."

Stepping back into the kitchen, he found a beer on the top shelf of the frig, popped off the bottle cap, and returned to the living room. After sitting down in the other easy chair across from her, he took a long swallow and watched her closely.

"I guess you rich now, huh?" he snapped.

Angela spread her hands, pleading with him. "I never expected this to happen, but I got lucky. Got to take advantage of it. You'd do the same if this happened to you. Sorry to call it quits with our business, but there's no reason for me to take those kinds of risks anymore. You can understand that, can't you? Nothing lasts forever. We both made some money, you got a house, and nobody knows what happened, so we can just walk away "

"Walk away? Looks to me like you're doin' all the walkin' and I'm back to bein' a dealer on the streets. How you s'pect me to live? I got a mortgage to pay. How am I goin' to do that whichout you?" he snarled. His eyes narrowed. "How do I know you won? You tryin' to get rid of me? Got a better deal with some other dude?"

Angela glanced at the end table, a look that did not go unnoticed by Art.

"I've checked it a million times. I understand you've got bills to pay. We've both got bills." She paused, as if an idea just occurred to her. "I'll tell you what. This last package, we're each getting twenty grand for it, right?"

He nodded.

"Okay, when you deliver it tomorrow, you keep all the money, my share, too." She spread her hands wide to show how generous an offer she made. "That's an extra twenty grand for you to help pay your mortgage until you build up your business again."

Art exploded. "Fuck you, Angie. You're gettin' millions and I get twenty grand? Then you go away and start a peaceful life on an island somewhere and I'm back on the street here, dealin' with the crack heads? It ain't right. My whole life I seen you get it all; college degree, legit job, the house when Dad died…I got nothin'. It ain't right! I deal drugs 'cause it's the only way I can make money. You got plenty of money now. Gimme a little. Then we both can walk away from this."

She stared back at him for a moment, chewing on her bottom lip. "Okay," she sighed, "Here's the best I can do. You keep the twenty grand. When I cash the ticket, I'll throw in another $200,000. That's enough to pay off your mortgage."

He waved a hand in dismissal. "Chump change."

Pursing her lips, she jutted out her chin, getting angry at his greed. "After taxes, I'll only get half of it. If I want all the money now, they discount it, so I'm only getting a third of the total. That's got to last me fifty years. It may seem like plenty of money, but it's not."

Art did some quick calculations in his head. "You still got 'bout forty-five million. You kick back a mil to me, and you got plenty to live on. Shit, you invest it right, you can live off the interest. I ain't askin' for much here, just 'nough for me to pay everything off and have a little left over for a fresh start. Get me out of dealin'.

It was a fair offer. She wouldn't even miss it, but it would be serious money for him. Pay off his house and have some left to buy a fast-food franchise where he would give the orders instead of kissing his sister's ass. No worries about getting busted every day. Never have to see a crack head again. *Does she even give a damn about me?* It took an effort he never knew he had to contain his anger while waiting for her reply.

When it came, it was full of contempt. "A million dollars *isn't much?* Easy for you to say when it's not your money. Remember, I won this on my own. You've got no right to any of it."

"You bitch!"

He sprang from his chair and reached for her throat. Caught by surprise, she scrambled to her right and yanked open the drawer on the end table, trying to grab her pistol. Just as her fingers curled around the grip, Art reached her.

Yanking the pistol from the drawer, she struggled to aim it at him. Her miscalculation had pushed him too far. It had become a fight for survival—kill him before he killed her.

His eyes grew large as he saw the pistol swing in his direction. He grabbed at it with his left hand, while the other closed on her throat. He was much stronger, but awkwardly draped over her body, which took away his leverage. They struggled for the gun. Angela couldn't stop him as he bent the pistol away until it pointed between them.

Her breath came in short gasps as he squeezed her throat. Soon she would be unconsciousness. In a last gasp effort to save herself, she squeezed the trigger. A shot rang out, and the gun fell to the floor. For a second, they both froze.

Then it was over.

Chapter Eight

Art staggered back and collapsed in his chair. His left ear hurt like hell. The pistol went off right next to it, and now all he could hear out of it was a high-pitched hum. Air whistled in and out of his lungs while he tried to slow his breathing. Checking himself for damage, he found blood on the right sleeve of his shirt, but he felt no pain. The rest of his body seemed untouched.

In a daze, he gazed at his sister. Sprawled back in her chair, her arms hung down on each side. A look of surprise was on her face. Her eyes were wide open, staring at him. A large blood stain spread over the front of her blouse.

He scanned the room, looking for the pistol, spotting it on the floor next to his sister's chair. The barrel pointed directly at him, as though to say it should have been him with a hole in his chest, not her. He was totally surprised when she pulled it out of the drawer and aimed it at him. She had never liked guns.

"Angie?" he whispered, hoping for a response.

All he got was a dead stare. There was no sign of life. When the stare became too much to endure, he rose, staggering to the kitchen sink. Turning on the cold water, he plunged his arms into it, rinsing off the blood, which was all Angela's. When the water ran clear, he cupped his hands under the faucet, splashing water on his face. The cold water had the desired effect, settling him down, wiping away the shock of what had happened.

Thoughts ran through his brain at lightning speed. It was an accident. Self-defense. Trying not to get shot. He never had the pistol. Angie pulled the trigger. He shook his head to clear it and returned to the living room to face the carnage. Gazing down at his sister, he avoided her eyes. The bloodstain covered the left side of her blouse, just below her heart. The shot must have killed her instantly.

"I'm so sorry, Angie," he said, and sat down and cried for a long time.

The need for self-preservation aroused him from his grieving. His watch told him, much to his surprise, that forty-five minutes had passed since the shot was fired. The police had not arrived, so he assumed no one had heard it.

He debated what to do next. One option, call the cops and claim self-defense. This, he dismissed immediately. They would ask what started the argument, as well as the contents of the locked bedroom. Then they would find out what he did for a living, and it would be over for him.

Option two, leave now, while it was dark outside. The brewing storm would be his friend, keeping the neighbors inside their homes. With luck, no one would see him leave. This made much more sense.

Stepping back, he studied his sister's body. If he left the pistol on the floor, the cops might consider it suicide; only Angela's prints were on the gun. Then he had a better idea. Take the pistol and make it look like someone killed her in a robbery gone bad. Give the cops a simple explanation for her death, and it was unlikely they would dig any further. He got to work ransacking the house, taking whatever valuables he found.

He debated what to do about the package. It wasn't possible to leave it there for the cops to find. An investigation would be launched, tracing it back, opening up a whole new investigation that might eventually involve him.

The package is worth forty grand, he reminded himself. No one would look for Angela's body for a day or two, so the handoff tomorrow bore little risk. After that, when her body was found, it would be gone, along with any evidence of their business venture.

He was ready to get it when he remembered the lotto ticket. Stepping over his sister's body, he looked in the open drawer of the end table where the gun had been. Inside, he spotted the corner of a plastic sleeve. Retrieving it with two fingers, he was careful not to touch anything else. After studying the contents of the sleeve, he smiled and placed it in his pocket.

He loaded everything he'd looted into the van before returning for the package.

"Okay," he mumbled to himself. "Time to go."

Chapter Nine

January 14th

Ron stared at the vending machine in the break room, wondering how long the Danish roll had been there. As he peered through the glass, searching in vain for an expiration date on the package, his stomach growled. After careful consideration of the possibility of food poisoning, he decided not to risk it.

He had forgotten to buy groceries yesterday, so when he went looking for breakfast, his refrigerator looked like the Sahara Desert. He vaguely remembered seeing a package of pretzels in his desk, which might appease his stomach until lunch. But who knew how long they had been there?

While pouring a cup of coffee to quiet his stomach, he remembered the LT's request for daily briefings. He added cream into the cup to mask the bitter taste and walked the short distance to Warner's office. It was quite spacious, designed to be shared by two people, although that had never happened. All that space was a boon for Warner, who found it difficult to throw away anything. Piles of books, equipment, an old set of golf clubs, and cast-off uniforms not worn in years took up most of the space. The janitorial service gave up trying to keep it clean years ago. Visitors were greeted with a musty odor of decay and thick dust.

"Welcome back. Been way too quiet around here," the LT said, grinning. His idea of a joke.

Ron gave a courtesy laugh, navigated around a stray nine iron, and plopped down in the chair opposite the lieutenant's desk. "Thanks for pulling us off mud duty, LT. That was the toughest job I've had since I put on the uniform. Then whaddya know, a routine ID turns into a murder."

Stone-faced, Warner nodded. "Fill me in."

The next half hour was spent reviewing what steps Ron had already taken, then a request for assistance. Angela Garcia's house needed to be searched carefully. To do that, somebody needed to get the mud out of it. He finished with a recap of his conversation with Art Garcia.

"Did you get any vibes?"

"Nothing specific. He didn't seem that shocked his sister was dead, but I'll have a better idea after I talk to him in person."

"Get him in here for the questioning so you can record it. I'll talk to Adams about getting the mud out of the house."

"Roger that," Ron said as he got up to leave.

Back at his desk, he called Angela Garcia's boss. "Mr. Rodriguez, this is Detective Jackson from the Santa Barbara County Sheriff's Office. If you have a few minutes, I'd like to ask you some questions about one of your employees."

"If this is about Angela Garcia, I was expecting your call. What a tragic accident. I had a bad premonition about her after she was a no-call, no-show for a couple of days. Angela would never take off like that. Totally out of character. I called Human Resources to report her missing when I couldn't reach her."

"How much do you know about the case?"

"Just what our HR people told me. She was found buried in a mudslide. I have told no one else about this, as requested," Rodriguez added quickly.

So much for maintaining confidentiality.

"I thank you for that," Ron said. "The investigation into her death is at a very early stage, and we don't want false rumors getting started. You know how the media can sensationalize things."

"Of course. I'll keep this conversation between the two of us."

"Thank you. I have a few questions. Was Ms. Garcia well liked? Did she have conflicts with anyone?"

"She wouldn't win a popularity contest, but she didn't have any enemies that I know of. Just did her work, didn't socialize with anyone," Rodriguez replied. "Angela never talked about her personal life. I know she was single, may have been dating, but that's just speculation on my part."

"What made you think she was dating someone?"

"Lately, she seemed happy about something. Like a different outlook on life."

Ron looked up in annoyance as two cops passed by his desk, laughing loudly at some joke or other. After a pause, he resumed his questions. "Sorry about that, sir. What exactly were Ms. Garcia's job duties and responsibilities?"

"She was my second in command. Kept the cases moving. When someone abandons a child or the minor is removed from the home, we get notified by the police. Angela would assign the matter to a caseworker, then start the paperwork. As one of the more experienced caseworkers, she took the hard cases."

"What do you mean by *hard case*?" Ron asked.

"Like a kid found with his parents dead and no relatives to take him. Or an abandoned baby with no ID."

Not something I'd want to deal with, Ron decided. "Would it be possible somebody she had contact with while handling these cases might have held a grudge against her? Perhaps even hated her?"

"She mentioned nothing like that to me. I suppose it's possible, though. Some parents might hold a grudge for having a kid taken from them, although it's the judge who decides that. Do you think her death had something to do with work?" Rodriguez asked. "Was she killed by one of the parents?"

"There are facts in this case which are not public so I'm not at liberty to discuss them," Ron said, deflecting the question. "Is there anybody else who might have wished her harm?"

The man's tone sharpened, sounding just a touch defensive. "Look, detective, I run a tight ship here. Everyone under my supervision is focused on their caseloads. I've never had any problems. You're wasting your time if you think Angela's death had anything to do with her job."

Ron thanked Rodriguez for his time, mentioned he might need additional information later, and hung up. Scribbling some notes in the murder book, he wondered why Rodriguez seemed so certain Angela's death had nothing to do with his department when he claimed to know none of the facts.

Yanking an abused or neglected kid from the home isn't a dangerous job?

Tell me another fairy story, pal.

He looked to the adjoining desk and saw Mary Ann

working through her emails. "Anything interesting?"

"Phone records is all. I'm printing them out, easier for me to see patterns. She called somebody early in the evening of January seventh. The last call recorded before her death. It's doesn't fit her profile."

"Why do you say that?"

She smiled. "I knew you'd ask, partner so I had the number traced. Guess what? It's a burner phone. Her phone records indicate she called this number often. Who do you suppose she contacted that didn't want to have their name known?"

He had the answer to this, as did Mary Ann. Criminals often used burners. Purchased with cash at convenience stores, they were completely anonymous. Many calls to the same number showed a long-term relationship with the person.

"Supports the druggie theory," Ron mused.

"It doesn't seem to fit. No arrest record, not even weed. Nobody we spoke to mentioned a drug problem."

"She was a loner. Drugs might have been why."

"Possible," she admitted.

"Let's get a subpoena for her bank records. See if she withdrew large sums of money. Any other numbers besides that one she called frequently?"

"Only one. She didn't make many calls. Seems to have led a rather solitary life."

"Traceable?"

"Yes. It belongs to a Patsy Stonehead."

"Why don't you work on the bank records while I see what I can find about her."

Swinging back to his computer, he entered "Patsy Stonehead, Santa Barbara, California" into the search box and got five matches.

The one that seemed the most promising—and most logical—belonged to an attorney, specializing in Family Law. Her website contained pictures of smiling parents and children, and a flattering one of herself. She'd graduated from the Loyola University School of Law in Los Angeles and established her practice ten years ago. Her office was in Goleta, the next town over from Santa Barbara.

He copied down the information. Next, he logged on to the California State Bar website through a portal available only to law enforcement, got everything the State Bar had on her, and hit pay dirt.

Eleven years ago, a previous employer reported her to the state bar association for embezzlement of client funds, leading to her law license being suspended for six months. There was no record of a criminal conviction, so her employer must have covered it up to avoid embarrassing the firm. There were no records of any other misdeeds since that time.

He pieced together what must have happened. An unethical lawyer caught stealing from a client would never be hired by another reputable law firm. Most likely she moved to Santa Barbara, where she was unknown, in order to survive. She practiced family law, which meant kids, and Angela dealt with kids. Perhaps they met in court and somehow became friends. Maybe Angela confided about somebody bothering her. Or they argued over something, so the lawyer shot her.

He compared her home address on file with the State Bar to the address attached to her phone number. They matched, so he had the right Patsy Stonehead.

During lunch, the detectives compared notes. Ron told Mary Ann what he found about Patsy Stonehead.

"Interesting," she commented. "She might tell us something. I got the subpoena for Angela's bank records. No unusual withdrawals, just her mortgage payment, utilities, car payment, and household expenses."

"Nothing to support the drug habit theory," he noted.

"The tox screen from the autopsy would show any drugs in her system."

At that moment, the LT stopped at their desks. "Anything new?"

Ron filled him in that he preferred having the autopsy and tox screen results before any in-person interviews with Patsy Stonehead or Art Garcia. If suicide became a possibility, the line of questioning would go one way. If a homicide was indicated, the questions would be different. The threat of a first-degree murder charge might lead to a confession.

The LT nodded, then snapped his fingers. "Almost forgot to tell you. Adams accounted for everybody reported missing, so he's going to take the mud out of Garcia's house tomorrow. It's beyond repair, so they'll take the roof off first. He tells me it's safer if they don't have to worry about it caving in."

The day shift ended, and the station emptied rapidly. The detectives joined the exodus. All day, Ron dreamed of sinking onto his luxurious mattress, which he had spent a month's salary on, and sleeping for a week. They piled into Mary Ann's car.

"Home, James."

"You better knock that shit off, or I'll let your ass off at the bus stop," Mary Ann snapped in a display of her low tolerance for being disrespected.

He raised his hands in surrender. "No offense. I'm

just glad to be getting home."

"I know it's been tough living out of that roach motel. I'm glad you're going home too, so you can drive your own damn car."

Mary Ann got on the 101 going south and drove past Olive Mill Road. By now, the freeway looked close to pristine, as if the mudslide never happened.

"Are you hungry?" Ron asked to make amends. "I'm buying."

"Well...There is this new place I've wanted to try down by the beach. I hear it's kind of expensive. How about we try it out ... sailor boy?"

"Really? I was thinking of something simple, yet wholesome, like Burger King."

"Fat chance. It's going to cost you big to ensure my silence this time."

Ron knew he was screwed. He mentally tallied how much money he had in the bank and gave her a stern look. "Okay, but I get to choose what you can order."

She laughed.

The new place was Chateau Lafayette, where the ambiance was outdone only by the price of the food. Mary Ann ordered four courses, including wine. Ron gulped when he received the bill.

It was close to nine before they arrived at his house, which looked forlorn in the darkness. She popped open the trunk, allowing him to retrieve his suitcase. He walked around to the driver's side of the car. "Beer?" he asked, pointing at his front door.

She hesitated. "Give me a rain check; I've got to relieve Mom. Can't lose my only babysitter."

Ron hid his disappointment. "All right, see you tomorrow, partner."

Waving goodbye, he fished his keys out of his pocket, and unlocked the front door. Inside, he flipped on the hall light, and noticed a musty smell from lack of air circulation. The sparsely furnished living room contained a worn couch, two chairs, and a coffee table. He walked past the kitchen, to the end of the hall, and turned left into the master bedroom.

Somewhat better furnished than the living room, it contained a queen-size bed, a four-drawer dresser, and two end tables, each holding a table lamp. On top of the dresser was a picture of a young couple, smiling into the camera. A young boy, dressed in a starched white shirt and black pants, stood in front of the man, looking resentfully toward the camera. A woman held a girl about two years old who had a blue bow in her blond hair and a pink dress. The resemblance was striking. A mother and daughter.

Ignoring the emotions evoked by the photo, he threw the suitcase on the bed then retraced his steps toward the kitchen.

Behind the stainless-steel sink, a bay window jutted out into a small side yard. A plant sat by itself on a shelf in the window. Claudia, his ex-wife, gave it to him as a joke before things went to hell between them. He thought of it as his surrogate dog, only better, because it didn't crap all over the yard. It was a reminder of the brief time in his life when he had it all.

He often thought of her with regret, wondering if they would still be together if he had tried a little harder to make it work. The stresses of the job, and stubbornness, came between them. Neither would make the compromises necessary to save the marriage. So now, he had no family. His father was dead and his mother was quickly sinking into dementia. He had no siblings. None that were alive, he corrected himself, pushing aside painful memories.

The plant looked the same as the day he left. Ron smiled, wishing everything in his life was as durable as the plant. He gave it some water, flipped off the kitchen light, and retreated to his bedroom.

Stripping off his clothes, he stepped into his oversized shower and let the hot water run over his body, helping to relax the knots in his shoulders. After fifteen minutes, he stepped out and toweled off.

As he fell asleep, his thoughts drifted to a favorite childhood game, cops and robbers, which he had played daily with friends. Ron always insisted upon being the cop, arresting everybody and throwing them into a "jail" built out of cardboard boxes.

He wondered, not for the first time, whether it had been worth it, following his childhood dream. The dream hadn't turned out to be what he expected. He gave everything to the job and got little happiness in return. Something important was missing from his life. Something he would never get from work. He didn't know what it might be, and that drove him crazy. Bouts of depression, which he used to shrug off, occurred more often now, and were impossible to ignore.

Was this some sort of sign, telling him to get out before the job destroyed him?

Chapter Ten

January 15th

Ron's alarm clock went crazy at six a.m. It was tuned to a heavy metal radio station which never failed to wake him regardless of how soundly he slept. He considered getting his gun out and shooting it but decided that would be a waste of a bullet since he was already awake.

The first night back in his own bed was the best sleep he had in weeks. With a yawn, he stretched and rolled out of bed. A peek out the window revealed an overcast sky, but no wind, typical for this part of California in January. After a hot shower which did wonders, he put on a gray suit and wandered into the kitchen, searching for something to eat.

His refrigerator once again disappointed him, empty except for a half full carton of milk and a six-pack of beer. If he didn't remember to go to the store soon, starvation was inevitable. After rummaging around in the pantry, he found a stale box of Maxi Crunch, his favorite cereal. Pouring a generous helping into a bowl, he drowned it with milk while flipping on the TV to catch the morning news. And there it was, the lead story: Angela Garcia found dead in the Montecito mudslides.

The reporter had the basic information. Cause of death would be determined by an autopsy. He breathed a sigh of relief. The reporter hadn't found out about the murder. Finishing his cereal, he rinsed out the bowl, and locked up the house. On the road by seven, he walked into his office before eight.

Mary Ann, as usual, was already at her desk, and frowned as he sat down. "Out of habit, I almost drove over to the roach motel this morning to pick you up. Then I remembered you left. I could have slept another half hour."

"Hope you got caught up on all that old paperwork, since you had so much extra time on your hands," he replied with a straight face.

She gave him the stink eye and waved at a large stack of files sitting on the corner of his desk. "Paperwork builds character. It would be off our desks by now except my partner, who works at the speed of a sloth, still has yet to do any of his."

"Those are mine?" he asked innocently.

"Yes, those are yours. You're making us look bad. If you want to keep the LT off your ass, you'd better wrap them up."

He grimaced at the pile of folders, grabbed his cup, and moved toward the scent of coffee. "There are more important things in life."

After his first taste of the bitter station house brew, he spent the morning digging into the old files, basically killing time while waiting for Alonzo to call with the results of the autopsy. Around ten, his phone rang.

It was the duty cop manning the front desk. "I got a caller who says she knows something about the Garcia case."

That got his attention. "Did she say what?"

"Said she wanted to speak with the detective in

charge of the investigation."

"Okay, put her through." He waited for the usual clicking sound on the phone before he gave his name and rank.

A female voice said, "My name is Jane Powers. I live, or I guess I should say I used to live, next door to Angela Garcia."

Her voice sounded weak and scratchy. He pegged her as somebody older and frail. "I saw the news this morning about her death. Did you find the child? The reporter didn't say a word about him."

Ron sat up a little straighter. "A child?"

"That's what I said, yes." Her voice rose an octave as though she expected him to know exactly what she was talking about.

"I'm sorry, Ms. Powers; did Ms. Garcia have a child?"

"No, no," she said impatiently. "I was driving home the day the storm hit, saw movement out of the corner of my eye, and glanced in that direction. Angela was in her garage, getting out of her car, and she had a little boy with her."

"On December seventh? Before the rain started?"

"That's right."

"Do you remember what time you saw them?"

"I was on my way home from my book club, which ends at three, so about three thirty."

"What did she do next?"

"Took the boy into the house," she said confidently. "I continued on up the street to my driveway, so I didn't see them after that."

Ron's interest ramped up another notch. "Had you ever seen her with this boy before?"

"No. I mind my own business. We seldom saw each other. Although—" She paused here as though reluctant to say anything more.

"What is it, Mrs. Powers?"

"When l saw Angela earlier this year, I think she had another child with her then…a girl."

"And she took this girl into her house?"

"Yes, she did."

"How old were the kids?"

"I'd say the boy was about ten. The girl, much younger, five or six."

"Did you ever see these kids again?"

"No. The only reason I remember is it seemed strange for kids to be with her. She didn't have any of her own. I know she lived all alone in that house."

"Did you notice anyone else visit her on December seventh, after you got home?"

"I can't see the front of her house when I'm inside my place, but I thought I heard a car engine later on after dark. It had gotten real windy by then, so I'm not sure about that. Did you find that poor boy?"

Ron sensed the worry in her voice. "There has been no discovery of another body. Based upon your information, I'll start another search of the area to see if we can find anything. Thank you very much for calling. If you remember anything else, please contact me."

Ron took down her phone number and address and gave her his direct number. Hanging up the phone, he blew out a deep breath.

"What?" said Mary Ann.

"There may be a complication. Come on, I've got to talk to the LT. I'll fill you both in at the same time."

As they barged into Warner's office, the LT looked

up from a file he had been reading. "What's up?"

"There may be another body in the Garcia house."

"What?"

"Just got off the phone with the neighbor," Ron said. "She saw Garcia taking a young boy into the house about three thirty on the seventh. Search and rescue needs to be careful taking the mud out of there."

Warner reached for his phone, dialed a number, and put the call on his speaker so the detectives could hear the conversation. "Jim, you start the Garcia house yet?"

"Roger that. I'm taking the roof off now."

"Be careful with the suction hose," Warner said. We got some new intel that there may be another body in there."

"No shit. All right then, we'll run everything through a sieve. Call you if we find anything."

"Wouldn't hurt to let the cadaver dogs sniff the area again, too."

"Got it."

The detectives went back to their desks and continued playing the waiting game. About two thirty, Alonzo called with the autopsy results.

"What did you find?" asked Ron.

"Shot once. The gun was small caliber, a .22. We retrieved the bullet. I'll send it over to ballistics. From the angle of the entry wound, it's unlikely she shot herself. Someone fired the gun from her right side, at an angle pointing down at her heart. No powder burns, so the shot came from at least a foot or two away. Never seen a suicide like that.

"We did find faint gunpowder residue on her right hand," he continued. "The mud messed up our forensics, so I can't say for a fact she was holding the gun when it fired or just had her hand near it."

"Might she have been fighting with someone?" Ron asked.

"Sure. A struggle for the gun or the shooter came up behind her and she raised her hand to protect herself."

"Estimated time of death?"

"Sometime between six and eight p.m."

"Just to be clear, the mudslide didn't kill her?"

"Correct. No evidence of asphyxiation, nothing in her lungs, no signs of blunt force trauma."

"Any drugs in her system?"

"None."

"Thanks Alonzo."

"You'll get the written report tomorrow."

Ron hung up and filled in Mary Ann. They talked about possibilities. The lack of drugs in Angela's body, along with no suspicious withdrawals from her bank account did not support the drug addict theory. Her death was not likely the result of a drug deal gone bad. With the coroner ruling out suicide, it was time to consider other possibilities and start interviewing suspects. Art Garcia, their prime person of interest, would be first. Next, would be Patsy Stonehead.

Ron was about to call Garcia when the phone rang. It was Pete Adams from Search and Rescue.

"Hey Pete, how they hangin'?"

"Still there last I checked. My guys finished pumping out the Garcia house. Real careful, ran all the mud through a sieve, but we found no body. However, we did find a large safe, locked of course."

"Excellent. Lots of secrets in a safe. You didn't find a gun, did you?"

"No. If there was one in the house, the sieve would

have caught it."

"Damn. Hoped we'd catch a break on that. Got a murder on our hands with this one. It's official."

"So I heard. Are you coming out?"

News travels fast on the cop grapevine.

"Yeah, we'll come out now, before it gets dark."

"If you can get a flatbed truck out here, I'll use my backhoe to load the safe for you."

"Deal. I'll make the call. See you in forty."

****

As Ron drove through Montecito, the town still looked like a war zone. Although the major roads had been cleared of mud, the destroyed homes and businesses sat there, giant mounds of destroyed dreams, sad evidence of Mother Nature at her worst. The cleanup would take years and likely turn into nightmares for insurance companies. The charming 1960s vibe the town once cherished would never return.

He parked near Angela's house, avoiding the gaggle of people milling around. Ron ambled over to shake hands.

"Welcome to Casa Garcia," Pete Adams said.

The house bore no resemblance to its previous condition. With the roof removed, the exterior walls were all that held the house together. Mud, sucked out by a huge vacuum hose, stood in an oozing pile thirty feet from the house.

"Can we go in?" asked Ron.

"Just don't lean against any walls," Pete said with a grin. "The whole place might fall down."

Picking their way through the muck and mire, the detectives approached the house. The front door was missing, so they stepped across the threshold into a hallway. The floor was slick with a thin coating of slime. A faint odor of mold and decay permeated the air. Mary Ann snapped pictures as they explored, making a rough sketch of the floor plan. They found the kitchen on the right side of the hallway. Cabinets dangled, ready to fall off of the wall with the slightest provocation. The stove sat in pieces in the corner, and the sink lay on top of a ruined countertop. They carefully looked through the cabinets, finding only broken china and glassware.

Beyond the kitchen, a low bar counter opened into the living room. A few ruined chairs, and a couch covered in mud lay scattered. Open gaps in the back wall marked where several picture windows once provided views of the backyard. Nothing of interest here.

Retracing their steps, they took a right down another passage. Nothing was left in the destroyed bathroom but the shower pan and toilet broken into small pieces. A gaping hole showed where the sink and cabinets once stood.

Farther on, a small bedroom had suffered less damage. Furniture—a bed and a table, covered in mud. A few broken children's toys crowded together in a corner. The door sagged on its hinges.

"The wave must have missed this part," Ron said. "It looks like the living room took the brunt."

Mary Ann opened the closet door. "No clothes in the closet. Must have been a spare bedroom. The toys back up the neighbors' story. Angela might have babysat for friends or something."

They tromped down the hall to the next room, much larger, with a ruined queen-size bed, walk-in closet and an attached bathroom. This had to be the master bedroom. Inside the closet, they found the safe. Almost as tall as Ron, it was about two feet deep and sported an electronic keypad on the front panel.

"Got your lock pick?" asked Mary Ann with a smile.

"That would be illegal, partner. I'm shocked you would make such a suggestion," Ron retorted. "Besides, I left mine at home. We'll just have a locksmith open it for us. Then, after I use my excellent detecting skills to analyze the contents of the safe, I'm sure the murderer will be revealed."

She rolled her eyes. "If it was only that easy."

Inspecting the rest of the house, which comprised two more bedrooms, did not take long. Both had suffered heavy mud damage but gave nothing of interest.

As they returned toward the kitchen, Mary Ann stopped at the first bedroom. "Did you notice this?" she said, gesturing at the door.

Ron peered at it. "I do believe it's a bedroom door."

She gave him the "you're an idiot," look, pointing to a deadbolt on the door. "No way to unlock it from the inside without a key. Doesn't that seem strange on a bedroom door?"

He inspected the inside of the door and confirmed her observation. "Good eye partner." Pointing to the window he said, "Notice the window has bars on it? Did you see any bars in the other rooms?"

"I don't think so. Let's make sure."

They retraced their steps again and found no bars on any of the other windows. Nor did they find any more deadbolts.

"If Angela had a kid here, we must assume someone took the kid before she died, since nobody found him," Ron said, thinking out loud. "Possibly the parents. But babysitting somebody else's kid wouldn't require a lock on the door or bars on the window. This looks more like a prison cell, where a kid would be confined until someone came to get him. The neighbor said she might have heard a car later on that night."

"It sure seems like a prison," Mary Ann agreed. "Did she take a kid home while transporting him or her to juvie hall or foster care? Do caseworkers do that?"

He shrugged. "Hell if I know. I'll have another talk with Garcia's supervisor tomorrow."

The sound of a large truck interrupted their discussion. Pete shouted their ride was here. After taking more photos of the door and window, they jogged out to supervise the loading of the safe.

Chapter Eleven

January 16th

It was three days since he'd spoken to Detective Jackson. With still no word on the autopsy results, Garcia grew more and more paranoid. To keep busy, he drove over after lunch to see his sister's house, parking some distance away to avoid attention. He hiked up Olive Mill Road with his dog—just another local out for some exercise—and listened to the faint sound of bulldozers moving mud off in the distance.

The ruins of Angela's house sat some distance from its foundation. There were no signs of the roof, only the exterior walls remained. An enormous mound of mud stood nearby, which he assumed had been pumped out of the house. All the evidence that might explain his sister's death as a robbery had disappeared with it.

On the way home, he appraised the situation. The cops, since he had no alibi for the night of her death, would soon target him as a person of interest. They would find no motive for his sister's murder, but the more they dug into his background, the more the consulting façade he used to hide his actual business of selling drugs would crumble. The result would be he'd end up in jail anyway.

Minor worry when compared to what would happen if they found out about his partnership with Angela. He still didn't see how that could happen. It only involved the two of them, and his sister wasn't talking. No evidence existed to suggest the two of them were working together. The burner phone, as well as her pistol, were now at the bottom of the ocean.

He needed a plan to steer the cops in a new direction, but nothing came to mind. Knowing nothing about Angela's personal life made it difficult. The only thing that might help was the lotto money. With the money in his pocket, it would be possible to disappear and start a new life far from California. But claiming it would give the cops an excellent motive for him killing Angela. All they'd need to do was prove she bought the ticket.

That would be easy. The lotto computer logged where and when every ticket was purchased. The cops would check the store's video surveillance tapes, which would have a perfect picture of Angela buying the ticket, not him. He could always say she bought it for him, but he doubted anyone would believe that lame explanation. It would be too convenient. Proof would be demanded, and he had none.

So tantalizingly close. God was paying him back for all the lives he had ruined, and the people he'd let down. He didn't deserve that. His entire life had been a struggle to survive, and now his one chance to fix it was slipping through his fingers.

To make matters worse, he had trouble sleeping. The nightmare was always the same. He stood near his sister's house, looking for her. A noise would cause him to turn around, and his sister's dead face would rise out of the mud, her icy hands touching his face. After waking up screaming and drenched in cold sweat, he'd stay awake for hours, afraid the nightmare would return if he went back to sleep. If he could get her cremated and then scatter her ashes far out in the ocean, maybe the nightmares would go away.

It was an enormous relief when Jackson called that afternoon.

"About time you called! I been waitin' three days."

"My apologies. Busy time for the coroner, but we got the autopsy results today."

"Are you all done now? Can I get her body?"

"The autopsy revealed something unexpected. Angela died from a gunshot wound, not because of the mudslide."

"What? Angie shot?" He was sweating now, and desperately hoped he sounded surprised. "When? Who?"

"That we are investigating. We need to talk to everyone who knew her. Do you have time today to stop by the station?" Ron asked. "Just routine questions."

"This is bullshit!" Art screamed into the phone. "You think I killed my sis?"

"No, sir, but we have to establish the whereabouts of everyone at the time she died. Like I said, it's just a routine interview. It won't take more than an hour. Since you're going to visit the morgue to identify your sister's remains, perhaps we could get this taken care of at the same time."

"I can get my sister from them?"

"The coroner will release the remains after she is identified."

Art thought about that and gave a heavy sigh. "I can come in 'morrow afternoon. What time can I see her?"

"I'll make an appointment for you at the morgue at one p.m. After that, we can get together. Will that work?"

"Yeah, one o'clock. I'll be there."

Garcia stared at his cell phone after the call ended, nervously tapping his foot on the floor, an old habit when stressed. He mentally reviewed everything he said to the detective. Had he slipped up anywhere? The face-to-face meeting with Jackson made him nervous but delaying it would only increase suspicion. He needed to play the part of the grieving brother, eager to find out who killed his sister.

Finally, he could claim his sister's body and get it cremated. There would be no memorial service. The faster he scattered her at sea, the faster the nightmares might stop. That was all he cared about.

Chapter Twelve

January 17th

The next morning, as Ron drove into work, the sun was a dim bulb through the fog bank that blanketed the coast. It was nerve-wracking driving through fog that hugged the road. With visibility cut down to a few feet, it led to more than one pile-up on the freeway. It took him twice the usual amount of time to get to work.

Once at his desk, he sipped at a cup of coffee while talking on his phone with Ricardo Rodriguez, who said it would be grounds for termination if any caseworker took a child home. That answered one question. The kid was not at Angela's house as part of her work.

Next on his To-Do list, he reviewed the deed transfer to Angela's house, recorded upon her father's death. In the upper left-hand corner appeared the name of the person requesting the recording, Scott Alvarez, Attorney at Law. A computer search located a phone number for the firm.

Ron called, identified himself, and in two minutes, was talking to Alvarez. He didn't remember Angela Garcia until he searched through his files and retrieved her paperwork, confirming he had recorded the deed.

"Might I ask a few questions about the estate?"

"It depends on the questions."

"Angela Garcia is deceased. This a homicide

investigation. My questions pertain to that."

A gasp sounded at the other end of the line. "Murder? Oh my God! Well, of course I'll help in any way I can. What do you want?"

"Did you serve as the executor of her father's estate?"

"That is correct."

"How many beneficiaries?"

"Hang on a moment." After a few minutes, Alvarez came back. "Only two beneficiaries, Angela and her brother Art."

"What assets did he have?"

"It was a pretty simple will: a life insurance policy for $100,000; $15,500 in cash, and the Montecito home."

"How were these assets distributed?"

"The son got the insurance money and the cash. The daughter got the house and furnishings."

"That doesn't appear to be a very equal distribution. The land itself had to be worth over a million, wouldn't you say?"

"Undoubtably. I asked Joe—meaning Mr. Garcia—if he wanted to do it this way, and he confirmed that he did. I never asked him why because it was none of my business."

"I get that. Do you remember Art's reaction when he learned his sister got the house, and he only got $115K?"

"As I recall, he got pretty upset about it. He made some accusations about her turning their dad against him. Then he got up and left."

"Did he make any specific threats against Angela?"

"No, he just left. I got the impression he didn't want to lose his temper in front of me."

"Did you have any further conversations with him?"

"I gave him everything he needed when we met, so I never saw him again."

"Did you have any further dealings with Angela?"

"I transferred title to the house into her name and later on I created a will for her."

"I assume you have a copy of it?"

"Of course."

"Who are the beneficiaries of her estate?"

"Just a minute. It's in another file."

In the background, Ron heard file cabinets bang open, then after a few seconds, bang closed. Alvarez came back on the line. "Her brother, Art Garcia, and a woman, Patsy Stonehead, are the beneficiaries."

Now we're getting somewhere. "How are her assets to be distributed?"

"Let's see…" The sounds of shuffling papers sounded on the line. "House and furnishings to Patsy Stonehead. Any remaining assets, including cash, to her brother."

"Did she itemize the remaining assets?"

"No, it's written in a way to give a broad description designed to cover everything."

"Do you have addresses for the beneficiaries?"

"Sure."

As the attorney read off the addresses, Ron copied them down in the murder book. "Did they receive copies of the will?"

"Not by me. Angela may have given them a copy."

"When did you last speak to her?"

A moment passed before Alvarez answered. "About a month ago, when she picked up the will."

"Do you recall her mood at the time?"

"I don't recall her being upset about anything, if that's what you're getting at."

"Would you do me a favor and hold off notifying the beneficiaries until we've talked with them? We'll call you when we're done."

"If it doesn't take too long," Alvarez advised. "As the executor, I have a duty to notify them."

Out of questions, Ron thanked him for his time and hung up. He turned and grinned at his partner.

"What?" said Mary Ann.

"Remember that other person on the phone list, Patsy Stonehead?"

"What about her?"

"Guess who's the primary beneficiary in Angela Garcia's will?"

"No shit. Now there's a motive for murder." She leaned back in her chair, contemplating the ceiling. "Isn't it strange Patsy hasn't been trying to get in contact with her? No calls, no messages?"

Ron nodded and looked at his watch. "We'd better get on the road."

****

An ancient woman wearing a thick pair of eyeglasses accented with rhinestones, inspected the two detectives who dared to enter her domain. She sat at the front counter, guarding the entrance against the unwashed rabble who might want access. She looked frail, ready to join the bodies in the refrigerators any day now. Nancy Ghost was her name, so of course she worked in the morgue. It was well known it was her second home. She'd been here for forty-two years, and basically ran the place.

Although her body looked to be decaying, her

memory was sharp as a tack. She knew every cop, firefighter, and paramedic in the city, and was proud of that fact. She could tell you the name of a person she hadn't seen in ten years, just by looking at their picture.

She gave a short, barking laugh. "Well, look what the cat drug in." Fixing her gaze on Mary Ann, one of her favorites, she smiled. "How's that baby doing, darlin'? Keeping you up all night?"

"He's a handful but sleeps most of the time. Must be the Jack Daniels I put in his bottle."

Ghost thought this hilarious, cackling for a few minutes until it led to a coughing spell. Mary Ann waited for her to catch her breath. "We've got a guy, Art Garcia, going to show up at one this afternoon to ID his sister. Don't tell him we are here, okay?"

"Don't you worry, sister, my lips are sealed."

Ghost shifted her gaze over to Ron—*not* one of her favorites. She considered him aloof and somewhat conceited for someone who had barely been born when she started working here. "Still hanging on to Mary Ann's coattails?" she asked, pointing a bony finger in his direction.

Ron opened his mouth, ready to put the old bag in her place, but Mary Ann intervened quickly. "He's taught me a lot."

Ghost squinted at him like he was a spider in need of killing. "Good God, why do I have to put up with these idiots," she mumbled to nobody in particular. Pushing a button under the counter unlocked the door to the morgue. "All right, Dick Tracy. Get your ass on in there. Mary Ann, you deserve better."

The two detectives beat a hasty retreat into the morgue. "What does that woman have against me?"

asked Ron in frustration once the door clicked closed.

"Word on the street is she had the hots for you about fifteen years ago and you stood her up on your first date."

"Jesus H. Christ! If you tell anybody that, I'll make sure no one ever finds your body."

"What?" she asked, all innocence. "It's not true?"

They proceeded down a tile lined corridor smelling strongly of disinfectant, and eventually came to a door bearing a sign: "All visitors must check in here".

It was a small room with no windows, containing a few metal folding chairs. A counter ran along the back wall, behind which sat a short, pudgy, bald man in a white lab coat.

"How's it going Junior?" asked Mary Ann.

The Uncle Fester look-alike behind the counter glanced up from his magazine. "Hey Mary Ann! Long time, no see. I heard you had a baby. Hey Ron," he said as he walked in.

"I did, a boy," she said. "My mom's taking care of him so I could get back to work. Look, we got a guy coming in at one to ID his sister. Don't want him to know we are here, but we want to listen in to what he says."

Junior nodded. "So you think this guy might be the perp, huh?"

"Possible, but at this point we're just looking at him as a person of interest. Want to see how he reacts when he sees the corpse. We need to set it up with security before he shows up."

"Sure thing," Junior said. "Follow me."

He scanned his ID badge on a reader mounted next to a door to the left of the counter. The door buzzed and unlocked. A narrow corridor with windows on one wall looked into another room where the bodies were kept in refrigerated crypts. Passing through another door, they entered the security office, where the cameras and microphones positioned throughout the area monitored activity. The screens were watched by a uniformed officer named Jerry Binderman.

After greetings were exchanged, Mary Ann told him what they needed. With a nod, he popped a thumb drive into a USB port on a computer. Junior turned to get back to his counter.

"Hey, Junior," said Ron, "can you stall Garcia for about fifteen minutes after the ID so we can hustle out to the parking lot before he gets there?"

"Yeah, no problem. He's got to sign for the release of the body. That should give you plenty of time."

Ron caught some movement on one of the monitors. Someone was entering the front door. He pointed to the screen. "Could be Garcia. It's show time."

Chapter Thirteen

Inside the morgue, Art Garcia stared through the glass window as a thin man wearing hospital protective garb wheeled a gurney towards him. He gazed at it fearfully, seeing only a lump under a white sheet. The thin man kept coming, rolling the gurney next to the window, watching for the signal.

Art saw his own haggard reflection in the glass. He'd endured a restless night of sleep, waking up once when the dog started barking, and again later, from a disturbing dream he couldn't quite remember. Seeing the face of his sister filled him with dread, uncertain if it might make the nightmares worse. It didn't matter. It had to be done before they would give him his sister's body. Cremation came next as soon as possible. Then the boat ride far out into the ocean. Then maybe, just maybe, he would exorcise her spirit out of his life.

"Are you ready?" the attendant asked.

He was not ready, would never be ready. *Play the part. You can do it.* Taking a deep breath, he nodded.

The thin man saw the nod and pulled back the sheet to reveal Angela's face. A quick glance was all Art had intended, but he could not look away. Her face practically commanded him to look at her, to see what he had done.

Her skin had a gray pallor to it except for bluish lips. The eyes were thankfully closed, and hair brushed straight back along her scalp, disappearing into the white sheet under her body.

An image flashed into his mind—the look of surprise on her face the last time he saw her alive. It pushed him over the edge, into the dark place where he lost control. An anguished groan rumbled out from deep down in his chest. Huge sobs tore from him, tears streamed down his cheeks and onto his sweatshirt.

He put his hands on the glass. "I'm sorry, Angie, I'm so sorry," he said, again and again, unable to stop.

After a moment, the attendant gently guided him away from the window. "Is there any doubt in your mind that is your sister, Angela Garcia?"

Art shuddered, wiping the tears from his eyes. "No."

"I'm sorry for your loss. Would you like a glass of water?"

"Jus' need to get out of here."

"I need to complete some paperwork, have you sign it, and then we're all done. I'll have you out of here in fifteen minutes."

Art paid little attention to what the tech said. He was reliving the night Angela died, hearing the fatal shot, telling himself over and over it was not his fault. But she still lay dead on a cold gurney and haunted his dreams.

****

Deep inside the morgue, the detectives watched the whole thing from the security office. Jerry recorded the whole incident, removed the thumb drive, and handed it to Mary Ann. After thanking him, the detectives hustled out the back door and drove around to the front of the morgue. Ron parked at a distance, watching the entrance. Both detectives relaxed, waiting for Art to appear.

Chapter Fourteen

After completing the paperwork, and frantic to escape the morgue, Art rushed down a silent corridor lined with white tile. Panic nearly overwhelmed him when he realized he took a wrong turn somewhere and was lost. He was about to scream for help when he spotted the "All visitors must check in here" sign that marked the way to the exit.

After bursting through the front door, he stopped and leaned against the side of the building, gulping fresh air, trying to slow his hammering heart. In his left hand, he carried a pile of papers, while wiping his eyes with his right. Nothing could have prepared him for the sight of Angela's body. Even in death, she still had command over him. But it had been a catharsis, allowing a release of the grief he'd carried around like a boulder on his back.

Relief was short-lived when he remembered his appointment with the police. He cursed himself for stupidly agreeing to meet without time to recover from the intensity of the event he had just been through. But there was no going back now—Detective Jackson would be waiting.

****

After Art drove away, Ron followed at a distance to see if he would keep his appointment at the police station. He did, and with light traffic, arrived in twenty minutes. The detectives drove past him and entered through the back door. They were waiting at their desks when the duty cop called, announcing Garcia had arrived.

Ron strode to the lobby, introduced himself, and escorted Art to an interview room, where he introduced Mary Ann. The room was windowless, painted an off shade of white. Because of poor ventilation, the room was uncomfortably warm and reeked with the odor of sweat. The main piece of furniture was a table bolted to the floor. Two chairs were placed on one side of it, and one on the other. A camera mounted near the ceiling monitored everything.

"Thank you for coming, Mr. Garcia," Ron began. "Could we get you a cup of coffee or water?"

"Yeah, some water would be good."

Both detectives left the room to get it, making a beeline for the computer on Ron's desk. Inserting the thumb drive, he fast forwarded the file to where Garcia broke down, sobbing. His abject apology of "I'm sorry" played. Nothing else proved to be of any significance.

"Nothing much there," Mary Ann said, sounding disappointed.

"He's sorry she died, or he's sorry he did it?" Ron asked. "Let's go do the interview."

They picked up a couple of bottles of water from the break room and headed back. Garcia appeared calm when they entered the room, but his eyes betrayed him, still red from crying. Ron passed him a water bottle. He and Mary Ann sat down on the other side of the table.

"Mr. Garcia, in a minute I'm going to start the recorder," Ron said. "Everything you say from then on will be on record to help us with the investigation. It doesn't mean we believe you're a suspect; it's just standard practice in a murder investigation. I'm also going to read your Miranda rights as required by law. That's routine too. Are you ready?"

"Let's get this done," he replied in a low voice.

Ron pushed the record button mounted under the table and stated the date, time, and the names of everyone in the room. Once he'd recited the Miranda warning, he said, "Please state your home and business address and your phone number for the record."

Art gave them the information, stating he worked out of his house.

"What do you do for a living?"

"I got my own business, consultin' work," he said slowly, carefully.

Ron looked at him, raising his eyebrows, signaling he wanted more.

"Distribution," he clarified.

"Distribution of what?"

"Like how to get stuff from one place to 'nother."

Ron traded glances with Mary Ann. "You mean like importing stuff from China?"

Garcia looked confused. "No man, China ain't got nothin' to do with it. It's all local."

"I see. So you advise companies how to transport their product around the country?"

He seemed relieved that somebody had explained it. "That's it."

"Okay. What's the name of your business?"

"AG Consulting."

How long have you been doing this?"

"A couple of years."

"That's a pretty complicated business you got there.

Did you start it all by yourself, or do you have partners?"

Looking uncomfortable, Garcia shifted his position on the chair. "It's all mine. What's dis got to do with my sister?"

"Sorry," Ron apologized. "It just interested me, that's all. Let's talk about Angela. How often did you see your sister?"

"We talked on the phone."

"So you never saw her in person?"

"Jus' for holidays."

"Can you tell us the last time you spoke with her?"

"Can't say for sure. Maybe a few weeks 'fore she died," he said vaguely.

"So around Christmas? Did you get together for the holiday?"

"Yeah, 'bout that time. We went out to eat," he said proudly, as though that was a major accomplishment.

"Did you call her, or did she call you?"

Garcia looked up at the ceiling and frowned. "Don't remember who called."

"Where would you call her?"

"Her cell phone."

"And how would she contact you?"

"Same way."

Ron glanced sideways at Mary Ann, who was pecking away on her laptop with a frown on her face. *What's she doing?*

"Do you have multiple phones, Art?"

He patted the phone on his belt. "No, jus' this one."

Ron leaned forward and placed his hands on the table. "So you would use this phone—" he pointed to Garcia's belt, "—to call her?"

A look of panic flashed across Art's face. "We goin'

to talk 'bout phones or my sister?"

Ron's eyes narrowed and bored into him. "We can come back to that. Just to be clear, you didn't call your sister, nor did she call you on December seventh, the day she died?"

"Don't recollect no calls that day," Garcia said.

"Where were you on the evening of December seventh?"

"At home."

"Anyone with you?"

"No."

Ron noticed Garcia's foot tapping rapidly under the table. A small cockroach, disturbed by the tapping, scurried around his shoe and disappeared through a crack in the bottom of the door leading into the room. "Go out that night?"

"No."

"Anyone vouch for you being home?"

"Jus' my dog," he said with a sneer.

Ron glared at him, then moved on. "You reported your sister missing on December twelfth?"

"That's right."

"So, what lead up to that?"

"I heard 'bout the mudslide over there, so I tried to call her, to see if she was okay. She never picked up, so I thought somethin' mighta' happened."

"Did you try to go to Montecito?"

"Yeah, but they blocked off all the roads."

"You try her at work?" Ron asked skeptically.

"I left her a message."

"Did you know she worked for Child Services?"

"Sure."

Ron abruptly changed the subject. "Did she ever talk

79

to you about her will?"

Garcia looked puzzled. "No, why would she?"

"So you don't know if you are a beneficiary?" Ron asked, casually leaning back in his chair as the heat built in the room.

"I jus' told you I don't know nothin' about her will."

"What would you say if I told you we spoke with the lawyer who made up her will, and he said he gave a copy to you?" Ron asked, bluffing.

Garcia glared at him. "I'd say he's a liar."

"Okay, we'll check on that. So when your dad died, he owned the home in Montecito, correct?"

"That's right."

Ron paused and noticed Mary Ann was absorbed in the conversation, no longer typing. "That's a pretty expensive area to live. The house had to be worth plenty of money, didn't it?"

"I guess," Garcia said with a shrug.

"Who inherited the house when he died?"

"Angie," he spat, bitterness in his voice.

"Just her?" said Ron, faking surprise. "You didn't get a share of it?"

"No."

"That doesn't seem very fair."

"Why you care? What's that got to do with her dying?" he snapped. Lines of sweat trickled down his neck, dampening his sweatshirt.

"It might be real important since the autopsy showed someone shot your sister."

"No shit."

Ron took another tack. "It's my understanding you and Angela are the only children of your parents, correct?"

"That's right."

"And she was single, with no dependents?"

"Yeah."

"So wouldn't it be reasonable to assume if she died, everything would be left to you?"

"How the hell would I know?" he said as he mopped his brow.

"This is a murder investigation. I'm just thinking of possibilities here, Art. Theoretically, if I was you and felt cheated out of my share of the estate, it might make me angry. And there is that million-dollar house, which would become mine if my sister died. There's a motive for murder right there."

"That's bullshit! We had a deal," Garcia shouted as he scraped his chair back on the linoleum floor and half stood, glaring at both detectives.

"A deal?" said Ron, unfazed by the shouting.

"She said I'd get forty percent when she sold the house," he said, while slowly sitting back down.

"Did she put that in writing, or was it just an oral agreement?"

"Jus' what she told me."

"Still, if you got one hundred percent if she died, that would be better than forty percent later, right?"

"I told you she never showed me her will!"

Ron appraised him, taking his time. Garcia was sweating through his clothes, his face flushed red. The air conditioning in the room struggled to keep up. "Okay, let's move on. Do you own any guns?"

"Three. I got a shotgun, a pistol, and an AR-15."

"What caliber is the pistol?"

"A .22"

"Are these guns registered in your name?"

"Yeah."

"Did Angela have a life insurance policy?"

"No idea."

"Did she ever talk to you about being afraid of someone, or someone who disliked her?"

Garcia looked down at his shoes, talking slowly. "She seemed kinda nervous the last time I saw her. Somethin' might o' been wrong then."

"Did you ask her about it?"

"Said she wasn't gettin' enough sleep."

"What did she mean by that?" *It's like pulling teeth to get any useful information out of this one.*

"Seemed somethin' was botherin' her."

"Did she ever mention the name Patsy Stonehead?"

Garcia smacked the side of his head. "Damn, she did mention that name. I forgot all 'bout it. Said somethin' 'bout not gettin' enough sleep 'cause she was nervous of Patsy."

"Nothing else about her?"

"She never talked 'bout her private life."

Ron sat back in his chair, thinking. Something felt phony about Garcia's business. Plus, he lied to them about his phone. Angela's call records did not show any calls from Art's phone. The information about Stonehead seemed fabricated, designed to point the finger of suspicion away from Garcia. Still no motive for murder, though. He nodded to Mary Ann who had her own set of questions ready.

"Were you aware Angela had a safe in her house?" she asked.

"No."

"It was found when we searched the house. Do you have any idea what might be in it?"

Garcia sat straighter. "No, but I'd like to find out."

"Good. We retrieved the safe and brought it back here to our evidence locker. With your permission, a locksmith could open it. Might be evidence in there that would identify the killer." Mary Ann was bluffing about this to observe Garcia's reaction. Since the safe was part of the crime scene, it could be opened without a warrant.

Garcia sat back, appearing to think it over. She could see he was curious about what might be in the safe. Would he risk giving them permission to open it, not knowing its contents? An innocent man would have nothing to fear.

"Well...uh...I'd rather open it in private. Let you know what's in there."

Mary Ann shook her head. "I'm sorry, but the safe might have evidence of the crime in it you wouldn't recognize. We need to be present when it's opened. Everything is inventoried."

Garcia fidgeted. "Got to talk to my lawyer 'bout it. Have him there, too."

Mary Ann spread her hands. "What's there to talk about? Something in there you don't want us to see?"

"You got no right to open it. It's private."

Mary Ann heaved a sigh. "Okay, Art. I think you're wrong about that. I'm disappointed; now I'm thinking you've got something to hide, and you're not being honest with us anymore."

He sat staring at the floor, foot tapping faster than ever, bands of sweat staining his sweatshirt at the armpits. The detectives stayed silent, waiting. Finally, he raised his head. "Are we done now?"

She returned his look. "Just a few more questions. The name of your business is AG Consulting?"

"Yeah. That's what I said before."

"How do you attract new clients? Do you advertise in some manner?"

Garcia hesitated before answering. "Word gets around."

"I'm really confused about how that happens. While you were talking with my partner, I did a computer search, and you don't even have a website. How does anybody know you exist?"

Panic came into his eyes. "Don't need no website."

Mary Ann glanced at her partner, who shrugged his shoulders. She leaned forward. "Okay, we're done for now, Mr. Garcia. But we may have more questions. Let us know if you plan to leave town for any reason."

Looking relieved, he stood, shook hands with the detectives, and pivoted toward the door.

"Oh, one last thing," Ron interjected.

Pulling his shoulders back, Garcia twisted back to face him. "What?"

"Why did your sister have a child at her home the night she died?"

Garcia froze, all color drained from his face. His mouth hung open in surprise, eyes darting around the room as if trying to find a means of escape. Drawing a deep breath, he sounded puzzled. "A kid? Why would she have a kid there? Where you hear that?"

Ron ignored the questions. "Are you sure about that? If you have some information, tell us now. If we find out later that you're holding back something, it won't go well for you."

Garcia leaned back against the wall, his face a mask. "Here's the thing. She took care of them kids all day; she don't want 'em 'round her after work. That's all I know."

84

Ron shook his head. "I don't think that's all, and we're going to prove it. We'll be talking again real soon." He opened the door, welcomed a blast of cool air into the room, and watched Garcia leave.

Disgusted, he turned to Mary Ann. "This case just keeps getting worse and worse."

Chapter Fifteen

It took every ounce of Art's willpower to walk, not run, out of the police station. The exit seemed a mile away. With each step, he expected somebody to yell at him to stop. Bursting through the front door, he came close to running over a person about to enter. Standing paralyzed outside the entrance, he couldn't remember where he parked. Then he saw his car, right where he left it, in the first row. He drove out of the parking lot still sweating, having no destination in mind, just needing to get away from Jackson.

A few minutes later, he turned onto a quiet residential street and parked at the curb. Overwhelmed with anxiety, his hands shook violently, and he could drive no further. His heart pounded in his chest, and he stunk from the sweat that drenched his sweatshirt.

The kid was the link to his sister that could bring him down. Jackson had caught him off guard with that question. His fear must have been obvious. The sneers on both cops' faces said it all. Both of them had the look that said they'd keep digging until they figured out the entire story.

Taking deep breaths, the panic slowly seeped away. Somebody must have told the cops they saw Angela with a kid at her house the day she died. The kid was always kept inside, locked in the bedroom, so how did it happen? Maybe she got careless. Left the garage door open when she took him out of the car, and somebody drove by and saw him. By itself, that would prove nothing. Since the detectives hadn't arrested him on the spot, it meant they did not understand *why* the kid was there. Without the why, they had no case. He was still untouchable, for now. That did not make him feel much better.

His thoughts drifted to the safe. What was in it? If Angela kept any written records of their business, it would be his doom. Unlikely, though, he concluded. Paranoia and secrecy were in her DNA. But it wasn't a sure thing. Better to keep the cops from opening it. Art made a mental note to find an attorney. He couldn't handle this himself any longer.

The questions about the will reminded him he needed to find it. Once he had that, he could get the property transferred into his name and sell it. Although the house had been destroyed, the land was precious, easily worth $800,000.

He needed more cash, now. The five thousand dollars a month mortgage payment on the five-year note, and all these unexpected other expenses were eating a hole in his savings. There had to be a way to get it.

Jackson tricked him with those questions about his cell phone. He admitted calling his sister with it without thinking. Stupid, stupid, stupid. But this didn't prove he murdered Angela.

He always used the burner phone to call her. There was no logical reason to give to the detectives that would explain it. He could never admit its existence. That would make him look guilty, and questions would arise why he used it. It would be obvious to anyone with half a brain that he was hiding something.

How was this Patsy Stonehead involved? She had to

be important. Jackson would not have mentioned her name otherwise. Why had Angie never mentioned her? He needed more information. Perhaps he could point the finger of suspicion at her.

A desperate hope, but it was all he had.

Chapter Sixteen

Ron slumped in his desk chair, sharing a bag of corn nuts with Mary Ann as they mulled over Garcia's interview. "So what was your take?"

She grimaced. "For starters, do you believe anybody would be dumb enough to hire him as a consultant? I don't think he knows diddly about distribution. And have you ever met a consultant who doesn't advertise? So he's likely laundering his actual source of income through this sham company he claims to own. I'm thinking it's gang related or drugs. He's not smart enough to be into anything more sophisticated than that."

"I agree, but does this have anything to do with his sister's death? That might imply he and Angela were in business together, and so far, she looks squeaky clean."

"Clean until you consider he lied about his cell phone," she pressed on. "Angela's call records show the only time he called her from it was after she died, like he was trying to establish his innocence. Yet he says that's his only phone. Why aren't there other calls to Angela from that number? Why did she never call him? We've got all her call records to and from a burner phone, and I'd be willing to bet my last dollar that's how they communicated."

"So they didn't want anybody to trace the calls," she continued after helping herself to a handful of corn nuts. "Why is that? The only explanation is they were doing some dirty business together. The burner phone would protect him in case Angela got busted. No way to prove it connected them."

"Without the phone, it's all speculation," said Ron. "And I'd be willing to bet he's tossed that phone in the ocean somewhere. He's not that dumb."

"He has no alibi for the night of the murder. Plus, he answered awful fast about where he was that night. Me?" she said, "I need a damn calendar to tell where I was last week, much less a month ago. And he's scared shitless about the safe. Got to get that thing opened."

"Of course," said Ron. "What's in there might bust this case wide open. I'll see about getting a locksmith out here to do it." Something else bothered him. "What about the kid? Did you see how he reacted when I dropped that on him?"

"Thought he was going to have a heart attack. He knows something."

"Maybe we're looking at this wrong. Their business might involve the kid, not drugs or gangs. If the kid was there just before Angela died, what happened to him? It couldn't have been a coincidence, like she was watching the kid for a friend, and the friend picked up the kid before Angela died. Art wouldn't have reacted like he did if that was the case."

"He said she didn't like kids around, too," Mary Ann pointed out.

Ron collected his thoughts. "She called the burner the afternoon she died. Let's assume it belongs to her brother. They have a conversation that causes him to drive over there. They fight over whatever she told him, so he kills her and takes the kid with him. The neighbor thought she heard a car later that night. Might have been him, leaving. But why was this kid there at all?"

"A kidnapping?" suggested Mary Ann. "Think he still has the kid?"

Ron shook his head. "I doubt it. Plenty of time elapsed for him to get rid of the kid before he reported her missing. That was the only thing that could tie them together."

"What did he do with the kid?" she asked, frustrated.

"Perhaps the ransom got paid, and he warned the parents not to contact the cops. We'd better go brief the LT, then check on any missing kids."

Chapter Seventeen

The detectives squeezed themselves into two chairs lodged in among the mess in the lieutenant's office. After being briefed, Warner said, "The media's been asking all kinds of questions about the case. They all have sources that feed them information. News of the murder investigation is going to leak soon. Set up an interview with Patsy Stonehead first thing tomorrow. Get to her before she hears it on the news."

"Roger that. I'll call her before we leave tonight," responded Mary Ann, stroking the lieutenant's ego.

"And start the paperwork to get a search warrant for Garcia's house. He admitted he had a .22 caliber pistol, and we've got the .22 bullet that killed his sister. So let's get his pistol and see if ballistics can match the two."

"One last thing LT," said Ron. "Can you authorize the expense of getting a locksmith out here to open the safe? Might be something in there that can help us."

"Yeah, that's no problem. Notify facilities and they'll get someone to do it."

Back at her desk after the meeting ended, Mary Ann retrieved Stonehead's phone number from the murder book and tapped in the numbers. When the call was answered, she said, "Ms. Stonehead, this is Detective Mary Ann McDonald with the Santa Barbara Sheriff's Department."

"Sheriff's Department?" She sounded surprised.

"How can I help you?"

"You may have some information that can assist us with one of our investigations. We'd like to meet with you tomorrow morning, here at the police station, to talk about it."

"What are you investigating?"

"The death, ma'am—of an acquaintance of yours."

"A death? You must be more specific. I'm not aware of any of my friends dying."

"Do you know Angela Garcia?"

There was a long pause on the line. "We are in the same line of work, and I see her in court once in a while. I didn't know her well. Is she the person who died?"

"Yes. We're talking with anyone who knew her to get as much information as possible, and I have a few routine questions to ask you. Could you meet me at nine a.m. tomorrow?"

"I'd have to check my calendar."

"Would you do that, please? I'll wait."

"Oh…okay…just a minute." There was silence for a few moments. Then she was back. "I've got an appointment at ten thirty; will an hour be enough time?"

"I don't want you to be rushed, so why don't we make it for eight thirty? Just ask for me at the front desk."

"I'll see you then."

Chapter Eighteen

January 18th

"Don't you ever sleep?" Ron remarked upon settling down at his desk the following morning and finding his partner, as usual, already hard at work.

"Of course," Mary Ann replied. "But unlike you old guys who need ten hours of sleep, I function well with only seven."

"I was up late talking to my succulent."

"What?"

"My *crassula ovata*."

Grinning, he got up to hit the break room for coffee. When he returned, Mary Ann was researching the word succulent. "A plant! You were talking to your plant."

"That's what I said."

"You made it sound dirty. Succulent sounds like a dirty word."

Shaking his head mournfully, he sat down and looked at his partner with great concern. "This proves that detectives who work with too little sleep become delusional. I suggest you get a cat nap before Stonehead shows up."

She gave him the finger and returned to her computer, muttering about the stupidity of the word succulent.

The lieutenant appeared at their desks. "Did you

guys catch the local news this morning?"

They shook their heads.

"Well, the cat's out of the bag. The media found out Angela didn't die in the mudslide."

"Shit," said Ron. "I hope this morning's interviewee hasn't seen it."

"Me, too," Warner said. "I've got a press conference at ten. If she is still here, take her out the back door when you're done."

Fifteen minutes later Mary Ann's phone rang, notifying her Patsy Stonehead had arrived. While she went to get her, Ron proceeded to the interrogation room. The women soon joined him.

Stonehead was a looker, dressed in a tight fitting, navy-blue pantsuit with a white silk blouse. Her shoulder-length blonde hair had been curled into a perm. A tan the color of mocha drew attention to her smooth skin. She acted every bit a lawyer, carrying herself with confidence. Mary Ann introduced her to Ron, then offered a chair. The detectives sat down on the opposite side of the table.

Ron stated the guidelines about recording the interview. Stonehead smiled, reached into her bag, and placed her own recorder on the desk. "I guess you won't mind if I record it too?" she said sweetly.

"Not at all."

The two recorders clicked on, the detective stating the date, time, and the people present. The Miranda warning came next.

"I have nothing to hide," she said at the start. "I will waive right to counsel for now. But I will refuse to answer questions which might infringe on the attorney-client privilege or my other rights."

"Thank you again for coming in on short notice," he began. "You stated on the phone you knew Angela Garcia through work?"

"My practice is family law, and she was with Child Services, so we sometimes worked cases together."

"What type of cases were these?"

"Cases involving children who were wards of the court. Most of the time, their parents were druggies, or they abandoned the child, things like that."

"How long had you known Ms. Garcia in this manner?"

"A couple of years."

"Did you interact with her outside of your court appearances? Socially I mean?"

Stonehead hesitated. "Well…we would sometimes have lunch together if we were both at the courthouse waiting on a judge."

Picking up on her body language, Ron asked, "Nothing more than that?"

She folded her hands together on the desk, eyes appraising her interrogator. "Before I answer that question, why don't you tell me what's going on? Why are you asking me questions about Angela? I was told on the phone this concerns her death."

"Okay," he replied. "Did you see the news this morning?"

She frowned. "No, I was rushing to get here."

"The reason you are here is that Angela Garcia didn't die in a mudslide. She was dead before the slide occurred; we are investigating her murder."

Stonehead sat back in her chair, a dumbfounded look on her face. Opening and shutting her mouth several times, she finally croaked, "Murdered?"

"Yes."

"But…but how?"

"Someone shot her."

Her impassive countenance turned to profound grief. Burying her head in her hands, she began to sob. Mary Ann handed her a box of tissues. After a few moments, she looked up at the detectives. "My God, that's unbelievable. She didn't have an enemy in the world. Who would do that?"

"That's what we're trying to find out. Now, will you answer my questions?"

She sighed. "Yes, there was more to… We, uh, dated for a while."

The room went silent as the detectives digested this bit of news. "So you had a romantic relationship?" Ron asked after a moment.

"Yes."

"And was this still going on at the time of her death?"

"We still saw each other once in a while, but it wasn't an exclusive relationship."

"So Angela dated other women?"

"I don't know; I never asked."

"So what you're saying is it wasn't exclusive on your part."

"Correct."

He bowed his head in thought for a moment and noticed another cockroach scurry across the floor. He wondered if it was the same one he saw yesterday. *Got to talk to the LT about getting this place fumigated. All these roaches are probably living in his office.*

He resumed the questioning. "Did Angela understand you were dating other women?"

"I think so."

"You *think* so?"

"Sometimes she would want to get together, and I would tell her I already had other plans, so I'm sure she figured it out."

Ron saw an inconsistency in her previous answers. "Initially you told my partner you didn't know Angela well. Why was that?"

"I didn't want all this personal stuff to come out," she replied quickly. "You didn't tell me the case involved murder."

Abruptly, he asked, "Where were you the afternoon and evening of December seventh?"

Stonehead rummaged around in her bag. "Let me check my calendar." Retrieving a tablet, she turned it on. "Okay, that was a Saturday. I had a late lunch with a friend of mine about one p.m. Then I went shopping at the mall for a few hours. I remember the weather started getting bad, so after that, I drove home."

"What time did you get home?"

"About five thirty."

Plenty of time to have committed murder.

"Did you go out again?" he asked.

"No."

"Can anyone vouch for your time at home?"

She reflected about it, then brightened. "I called my mother that night and talked to her for quite a while."

"Was that on your landline?"

"No, my cell. I don't have a landline."

"It's going to be necessary to subpoena your phone records."

"I have nothing to hide."

It was growing warm in the interrogation room

again. A thin film of sweat covered Stonehead's brow.

Ron continued. "Do you own any firearms?"

"I have a .22 caliber semi-automatic pistol."

Does everybody own one of these?

"When was the last time you fired it?"

"A couple of months ago when I visited the range to practice."

"Would you consider yourself to be a good shot?"

"I keep it for self-defense. I don't have time to practice with it very often."

"Can you give us the names of Angela's other friends?"

"This is going to sound mean, but I don't believe she had any friends. She was a very complicated person."

Ron's interest picked up. "How so?"

Stonehead hesitated, then said, "Someone screwed up her life when she was young. She never got over it."

"What happened?"

"She wouldn't talk about it. Her personal life was a secret, even from me."

Ron made a mental note to follow up on this. "So how did you two become so close?"

"It just happened. She discovered she was gay."

"So you were her first female partner?"

"Yes."

"Did she ever date men?"

"Not to my knowledge."

"She ever mention having trouble with someone threatening her?"

"To my knowledge, she didn't have any enemies."

"Did she ever talk about her brother, Art?"

"No."

"Do you know him?"

"No."

Ron stopped momentarily as the air conditioning unit rattled to life and blew lukewarm air into the room. It did little to make the room more comfortable. Patsy seemed unaffected by the heat, while Ron could feel sweat trickling down his chest.

"How long have you been practicing law in Santa Barbara?" he continued.

Patsy shifted to a more comfortable position in her chair. "About ten years."

"Family law the entire time?"

"That's right."

"What made you take up practice here?"

"Santa Barbara is a beautiful place, and there weren't many family law firms up here then," she said with a smile.

"It's a great place to live, but pretty expensive. Must be hard to make ends meet some months."

"My practice is doing well."

Ron decided to see if he could rattle her. "Better than it was four years ago when you declared bankruptcy?"

She glared at him. "I hit a rough patch when the economy wasn't doing well."

"Did you ever borrow any money from Angela?"

"Of course not," she said, waving a hand in dismissal.

The air conditioner suddenly stopped blowing air. *Jesus,* thought Ron, *the fucking thing only cooled it down about one degree in here.*

He eyed Patsy who now looked a little uncomfortable herself. "Have you ever seen a copy of her will?"

"No."

"So you didn't help her write it?"

"Why would you ask that?"

"Just wondering, since she named you as a beneficiary."

"She did?" she said, sounding surprised.

"Yes, she left you the house and the furnishings."

She teared up again, dabbing her eyes with a tissue. "That poor, misunderstood girl. I didn't realize I meant that much to her."

"The land could be worth a considerable amount of money. The estate will have to be settled. It's just you and her brother. So your law practice is doing well?"

"What are you getting at?" she asked, a new sharpness in her tone.

Ron went in for the kill. "There was that bankruptcy you had four years ago. It takes most people a long time to recover from something like that. Then that issue with your previous employer when you embezzled your client's money. Isn't it difficult to attract clients with that hanging over your head? Just thinking, theoretically of course, that someone who needed money, and knew they were the beneficiary of a lucrative estate…might attempt to cash in on that legacy."

She stiffened. "I think we're done here."

Mary Ann spoke up for the first time. "What's in the past can stay in the past, but if the press finds out you knew Angela, they might dig into your relationship with her. They like to sensationalize everything. If you've got anything to tell us that might help find the killer, now is the time to speak. For instance, you could tell us why Angela had a kid at her house the night she died."

Stonehead sat back in her chair, a stunned look on her face. For the first time, she visibly struggled with her composure. She opened her mouth to speak and closed it without saying a word. Pushing her chair back, she fixed the detectives with a gaze that could have melted steel. "I did not kill Angela. And if I find you leaked my name to the press, I will sue you and the county for every nickel you have."

Putting her recorder away, she stormed out of the room.

"That went well," said Ron.

Mary Ann grinned. "You forgot to tell her to leave by the back door. I hope those reporters at the press conference don't recognize her. You don't have very many nickels."

****

"I'm not seeing her as the killer," Ron said, gazing out his office window at a large squirrel running across the lawn. "If the time of the call to her mother was after six and continued for a while, it might clear her. Nobody kills someone while talking to your mom on the phone. And she seemed pretty broken up about Angela's death. It's hard to fake that."

"She gave us that nugget about owning a pistol, which is the same caliber that killed Angela."

He waved his hand in dismissal. "Those .22 pistols are as common as rocks. But if we strike out with the search of Garcia's house, we can always use that information to get a warrant to search her house."

He paused, taking a sip of coffee and grimacing at its taste. "The background she gave us might be important. I don't think anybody knew Angela was gay. If she hid it when she was young, maybe her parents found out and made her life miserable. Stonehead said she had some issues when she was a child, and her brother said she didn't like kids, so why did she work for Child Services? Was she so messed up she mistreated the kids she pretended to protect? Revenge for what she went through?"

"If she had problems at home, wouldn't Art be aware of it?"

"You would think so. He's a few years younger than Angela, but old enough to have known what was going on. What about the relatives? Aren't there a few aunts and uncles still alive who could shed some light on it?"

Mary Ann consulted her notes. "One aunt, Rosa Hernandez, who lives in a retirement home in Goleta."

"Let's go talk to her after we toss Garcia's house. Did you notice Stonehead didn't ask one question about the kid? If she wasn't aware of it, wouldn't she have asked me what I was talking about?"

"I caught that. too. She had that same look on her face as Art did."

"Are they all in this together?"

"We've got no proof Patsy and Art even know each other," countered Mary Ann.

"True, but they both had the same reaction to the question about the kid. Let's subpoena her phone records for the last six months and see if we can find a connection. Meanwhile, I've got to call facilities to get that safe opened."

Ron had just finished talking to them when the lieutenant breezed past on his way back from the press conference.

"How'd it go, LT?" Ron asked. "Did the press solve the case for you?"

"A bunch of real geniuses in there. One of them asked me if I thought it was a serial killer. Why are you guys still here? Didn't you get the warrant?"

"Nothing yet," replied Mary Ann.

"Christ. How the hell are we supposed to do our jobs when the DA can't do theirs?" said Warner. "Give Anderson a call and find out what the holdup is. When are you getting the safe opened?"

"I talked to facilities this morning, and they promised me a call back on that today," said Ron.

The Lieutenant sighed. "Well, this is just a murder case, so I guess nobody is jumping through hoops to help us. If you don't get any answers today, let me know."

After the LT left, Mary Ann called Sheila Anderson, the Assistant District Attorney for Santa Barbara County, who handled all police requests for search warrants. "Hey Sheila, did you process that request I sent over for a warrant to search Art Garcia's house?"

"Yeah, I typed it up first thing this morning and sent it over to Judge Donner. Nobody called you yet?"

"Nope. The LT is all over my ass to get it done."

"Alright, let me make a phone call."

Fifteen minutes later Mary Ann's phone rang. It was Judge Donner's clerk, apologizing for the delay. "The judge forgot about it before his morning cases, so I had to wait for the lunch recess to get his signature. Do you want to pick it up now?"

It was late afternoon by the time Mary Ann made it to the courthouse to pick up the warrant, too late in the day to start the search. Ron notified the team, composed of two other cops and two techs from forensics, to get ready. Everyone would meet in Santa Maria tomorrow morning and caravan to Garcia's house.

Chapter Nineteen

Art Garcia was at Mendoza's Mortuary, talking to a man in a black suit, completing arrangements to cremate Angela's body. The price was three thousand dollars, which, of course, he needed to pay up front. The suit did his best to sell him add-ons, like an urn for her ashes. He declined everything. Money was tight, and a quick scattering of the ashes at sea was his plan.

With the arrangements made, he went home, sat at his kitchen table, booted up the computer, and used the Yelp app to help him find a lawyer. The feedback on Jim Burnside was favorable. Four stars out of five. His office was close by in Santa Maria. Initial consultations were free. Art picked up his phone to make an appointment.

The attorney practiced in a three-story office building filled with other lawyers and accountants. Garcia introduced himself to an office clerk who gave him a stack of paperwork to complete. When he finished this, he was escorted down a corridor to Burnside's office, passing by several other offices where the indistinct murmur of conversation carried out into the hall.

The lawyer rose from his chair and introduced himself. Beneath a mop of uncombed brown hair, a pair of wire-rimmed glasses framed his hazel eyes on a round Charlie Brown face. Art was reassured to see the man dressed simply, in a long sleeve beige denim shirt and black slacks. He was always intimidated by guys who wore expensive Italian suits to work.

Sitting down in an overstuffed chair, Art ran through the highlights of his story. "So have I got anything to worry about here?"

"Here's my opinion," Burnside said. "Based on what you have told me, all the evidence the police have is circumstantial. It doesn't tie you to anything. I'm not saying they couldn't charge you with something, just that it would be difficult for them to get a conviction."

Art felt a little better hearing this. His situation might not be as bad as he thought. The story of the safe which the cops found in Angela's house was the next topic. "Can you keep the cops from opening it?"

"The answer to that is no. It's part of the crime scene, so they don't need a search warrant. The best I can do is petition the court to have the safe and its contents returned to you after they open it, assuming you are named in your sister's will as the owner. Do you have a copy of her will?

"Not yet. I got to find the lawyer that wrote it."

"That is unfortunate. You don't really know what your rights are until your sister's estate is probated."

"I don't know what's in that safe," said Art. "That's what worries me."

Burnside placed his elbows on his desk and made a steeple with his hands. "You may be worrying about nothing. Meanwhile, do not talk to the police again without a lawyer present. It appears they have zeroed in on you as their prime suspect, so do not give them anything else to hang on you."

"So what do I do?" Art asked.

"If they show up at your house with a search

warrant, make sure they give you the warrant before letting them search. Do not interfere with them. It might be best to stay outside the house during the search to avoid confrontations. They may try to goad you into saying something they could use against you."

The attorney sat back in his chair. "Should you wish to hire me, my hourly rate is four hundred dollars. I will need four thousand dollars now as a retainer. When that's exhausted, I'll need to ask you for additional funds to cover my expenses. Questions?"

This was the first time Art had talked to a lawyer his entire life, and he was shocked they got paid so much money. The lawyer's fees alone could wipe out his bank account. Between the mortuary and the lawyer, seven thousand dollars—over one quarter of the bonus money he'd earned on delivery of the last package—would disappear like smoke from his bank account. He needed more money. It was there, just out of reach, and driving him crazy.

Regardless of his financial problems, Art recognized he needed a lawyer. Things were getting too intense with the police. One mistake and he would end up in jail for a very long time. He agreed to hire Burnside. It was time he started fighting back.

Chapter Twenty

January 19th

The detectives were in the first car, followed by a second unit containing two more uniforms, and a third with two forensics techs. They turned off the main road onto Garcia's driveway and crept toward the house. A dog barked in the front yard but did not approach. Parking the car, the detectives marched toward the house, keeping an eye on the dog. Ron banged on the door, announcing the police had come to call.

After a moment of silence, the deadbolt turned. The door swung open to reveal their suspect, hair disheveled, standing barefoot in blue jeans and a black t-shirt. "What do you want?"

"Art Garcia, we have a warrant to search your premises. Please step aside and do not impede our work, or I will arrest you," Ron replied.

"Show me the warrant."

After Mary Ann handed it to him, he took his time reading it, then opened the door and stepped aside. Directed to sit in his rocker on the front porch, he remained calm as one cop kept watch over him. The remaining five filed down the hallway to the back of the house and started searching.

Two hours later, with the search almost completed, all they had found were three guns in a closet. Garcia's

.22 caliber pistol was one of them, and it was placed in an evidence bag.

There was nothing left to search except the kitchen and the garage. Since the kitchen was too small for all of them, Mary Ann took the kitchen while Ron went into the attached garage.

After opening the door, he found two vehicles parked side by side. The first he recognized as the sedan Garcia drove to the morgue. The second was an old, beat-up delivery van. He searched the car first, emptying the glove box and popping open the trunk to search around the spare tire. Finding nothing unusual, he focused his attention on the van.

The side door opened smoothly. He stuck his head inside and looked around. A roll of shiny duct tape lay on the floor. Someone had welded a steel mesh screen between the front and rear seats. The rest of the van looked empty. As he tried to shut the door, he discovered there was no door handle on the inside. Anyone riding in the back could not exit the van until someone from the outside opened the door.

Convinced this was not a coincidence, he retreated into the house, and found Billy, the lead forensics tech. "There's a van in the garage. I want you to dust the interior for fingerprints before we leave. And there's a roll of duct tape on the floor. See if you can get any prints off of that, too."

Billy nodded. "No problem." He turned and exited out the front door to get his kit out of his car. Ron followed him, intending to question Garcia.

As he walked onto the porch, he heard a familiar chop-chop and glanced up. A helicopter with the distinctive paint job of Channel 8 hovered a few hundred feet in the air, situated so its powerful camera could see an ant crawling across the lawn. Realizing the helicopter would not be here by itself, he walked off the porch, jogged across the front yard to the edge of the hill, and looked down to the main road. Vans from all the local TV stations jockeyed for position near the driveway. Their antennas extended up into the sky like probes, linking to their studios in town.

Shit. Now he would have to drive through a mob to get out of here. Somehow, the media always found out about search warrants. They probably bribed some clerk at the courthouse to call them. A big story would be on the evening news, and everyone would hear about Art Garcia. He thought about that, smiled, and went back to the porch.

"Noticed you have three guns in the closet. Are they all registered?"

"Yeah," he replied.

"Buy trigger locks or get a gun safe for them. It's illegal to have guns sitting around unsecured. And ammo needs to be stored separate from the guns."

"Ain't nobody livin' here but me," he said.

"Doesn't matter. It's the law. Get it taken care of before an accident happens."

Ron turned and went back into the house, through the kitchen, into the garage. The entire crew was in there poking around, watching the techs dust the van.

"There're a hundred fingerprints in here," Billy said as he stepped out of the van.

"Look for small prints, like a kid would make."

Eyes widening in comprehension, Mary Ann nodded. By the time they finished the van, it looked like a snowstorm had hit.

"We got a few prints from small fingers—like those a kid would leave," Billy said.

"Excellent work, people," Ron said. "Let's call it."

Everyone trooped out to the porch. Ron kept his face impassive. "Mr. Garcia, we have finished our search. We are confiscating your pistol as possible evidence in our investigation. Here is a receipt for it. You may go back inside whenever you like. Good day." He turned quickly and walked away before Garcia could protest.

Before they left, Ron pulled Billy aside. "Try to isolate the kids' prints first. Run them through the databases to see if we can get a match. Then check if any of the adult prints match Angela Garcia's or any known perps. Call me as soon as you get the results. I got a feeling about this."

At the bottom of the hill, Ron drove the car into a gauntlet of reporters, screaming questions and searching in vain for an open window to stick their microphones into. He kept inching through the crush until he met the main road, accelerating away from the crowd. The other two cars were right behind.

The drive back to the office was very subdued. Neither detective had much to say. The search had not gone well. Other than the possibility of a fingerprint match, or a match to the murder weapon, they had found nothing.

Chapter Twenty-One

June 1988

Bob Hackman joined the Army right out of high school, hoping to leave unpleasant things behind in the small municipality of Petersville, where he grew up. One of those things was Karen, a fifteen-year-old he had sex with regularly. Being the daughter of the richest man in town and under the age of consent, should have been enough to warn him away. But at eighteen, getting laid overruled the danger signs.

She was pretty with blonde hair, blue eyes, and a figure more common to someone five years older. The two of them started dating near the end of the school year. Bob sensed she was impressed that a senior would take an interest in her. The mating dance began, and soon they had sex at every opportunity. He believed her when she claimed to be on birth control. That was a lie.

"I need to tell you something," she said, lying naked beside him in the backseat of his Mustang on a hot night in August.

He was only half listening to her, thinking of the keg of beer waiting at his best friend's birthday party. First, he needed to smuggle her back into her house, up the trellis she had climbed down earlier.

"Babe, are you listening?"

He hated it when she called him that. There was no

emotional attachment to her. "What?" he replied curtly.

"I think I'm pregnant," she said in a small voice. "We're going to be parents."

Bob erupted. "What the fuck! You said you were on the pill, so how did you get pregnant? Lied to me, didn't you! Fifteen years old. What do you know about taking care of a baby? You're still a kid yourself. Are you trying to trap me into your fantasy world? It ain't going to happen. I've got plans and they don't include raising a baby. You and I are finished, understand? I don't want to see you or your baby again."

She started sobbing a river, but that just made him madder. He threw her and her clothes out of the car and burned rubber, leaving her there to find her own way home.

The next day, he enlisted in the army. It was the easiest way to escape the wrath he knew was coming when the richest man in town found out he had knocked up his little girl. The army sent him to Fort Polk, Louisiana, for basic training, a thousand miles away from Petersville. He felt safe there, but a month into basic training, he came close to being discharged for insubordination. A drill sergeant, who saw something in his character he liked, intervened on his behalf.

Bob was grateful. "Thanks for getting me out of that jam, sarge. I would have been in some deep shit at home if I got kicked out of the army."

The sergeant talked about Ranger training. "This is what you need, son. Rangers are confident, powerful men. Want to become somebody? This is the way to go."

Bob took his advice and soon found himself in a snake infested swamp in North Carolina learning to survive on nothing. The swamp smelled like a rotting garbage dump. Every night he heard a strange sound, a cross between a lion roar and a howler monkey, which made him want to get the hell out of there. He had no desire to find out what it was.

In six months, he turned into a stone-cold killer, trained in special ops and jungle warfare. When Saddam Hussein decided Kuwait belonged to him, Bob was part of a mission sent behind enemy lines to gather intelligence and create chaos. He excelled at interrogating captured soldiers, although his methods sometimes went beyond what regulations allowed.

He fought his way into Baghdad during the second Iraq war, narrowly missing being killed on a failed mission to capture one of Hussein's sons. The Army censored him for not following orders, but because he rescued two wounded Rangers, he kept his rank. Next, he deployed to Afghanistan. Bad things happened there that he would dream about for the rest of his life. When it was time to reenlist, he got out of the army, disillusioned with what it had made him.

Upon returning home, he found there wasn't much demand for stone-cold killers in the job market. Wandering the country, he did stints as a bodyguard for powerful people—not always law-abiding types. PTSD and alcoholism came close to destroying him until a friend referred him to a business that needed a man with his particular skill set.

The new job saved his life. He became a respected member of the team. The company relied upon him to complete tough assignments an ordinary person would not do. Most of them were illegal. He did not question the morality of it. A team stuck together, did what it had to do. Just like it had been in Afghanistan.

Chapter Twenty-Two

Garcia watched the cops leave, trailing a cloud of dust behind their vehicles. Sitting on his porch, he rocked back and forth for a while, pleased he'd outsmarted them. He had heeded his lawyer's warning about the search warrant and spent yesterday sanitizing his house to remove any evidence of drugs. The burner phone was long gone, so there was no danger of them finding that, either. Knowing they would find nothing helped him remain calm while his home got torn apart.

He was unfazed by the cops taking his pistol. It wasn't the one that killed Angela, so when the ballistics didn't match, they would have nothing. He rocked back and forth for a few minutes more until he heard a commotion coming from the road in front of his house. Puzzled, he rose from the rocker and walked to the edge of his yard. The side of the road was completely occupied by news vans and people with microphones staring up at him. Powerful flood lights snapped on, blinding him. Questions were being shouted. Shielding his face from the light, he staggered back to his house, rushed inside, and slammed the door.

There were reporters down the hill who wanted a story. He hadn't considered the media getting involved. Jackson probably tipped them off, just to fuck with him. Publicity in his business was bad news. It would scare off customers, making it even more difficult to survive.

He had no intention of talking to the reporters, so his only option was to wait them out. Who knew how long that would take.

Sighing, he surveyed the mess the cops left behind. Starting in the living room, he put drawers and cushions back where they belonged, working his way back toward the bedroom.

It was getting dark when he ventured into the garage. The smell of gasoline fumes from his lawn mower permeated the air. Flicking on the florescent ceiling light, he saw the trunk of his car open and the spare tire lying on the garage floor. Scowling, he heaved the spare back into the trunk and slammed the lid shut.

He walked over to the driver's side window of his van and peered in. All appeared to be normal except for the contents of the glove box being strewn on the front seat. It wasn't right that cops could throw things wherever they wanted and leave. There ought to be a law that made them put everything back the way it was.

He opened the passenger door and put his papers away. The cops left the sliding door to the back open, so he grabbed hold of the door handle to close it. Glancing inside, he was stunned to see the interior covered in white fingerprint powder.

Realizing the ramifications, he slammed his fist on the van's roof. It hurt like hell, but that was the least of his problems now. The kid had been in the van, and he touched things. A fingerprint from the van matching a set the cops already had, would give them the name of the kid. Once they had the name, the kid could be traced, and that might point to his sister. And from there, it was an easy jump to him.

Even without a link to Angela, the prints would

prove the kid was in the van. He could hear Jackson now. *"Please explain to us what happened to little Johnny? He seems to have disappeared, yet his fingerprints are all over your van."*

Garcia trudged back into the kitchen. The earlier smugness was replaced by panic, along with a new emotion, despair. He felt like a man on death row, watching the days go by, waiting for his execution. How could he have forgotten about fingerprints?

Rolling a joint, he sprawled on the sofa in his living room, clicking on the TV to see the news. The lead story was the search of his house. Unfortunately for him, the most exciting news item that happened that day. The reporter's story contained a lot of conjecture, because the police had no comment about the search. But, the reporter noted, Art Garcia is Angela Garcia's *brother*, so there might be a connection to her murder.

The reporter gave the name of the street he lived on, but not his actual address. Instead, there was an aerial view of his house, taken from the helicopter, with people milling around outside while he sat on the porch.

He sank deeper into despair. His name was out there now, and some of his wealthier clients would think twice before calling him. There were others they could buy product from who weren't being investigated for murder. No need to call attention to themselves by being seen with the likes of him. Plus, reporters would continue hounding him. Conducting business while being followed by a pack of them was impossible.

He owed five thousand a month on his mortgage, and without his drug sales, he had no income. His life was spiraling down to nothing. That was also the grand total of what he would have left when this was all over, he thought bitterly, whether or not he got arrested.

There was money in his sister's property, but it would be months before he could sell it, and he still needed to find the will. Angela might have some life insurance through her work, but he didn't know how much, or even if he was the beneficiary. He would have to find the right person in the vast county bureaucracy to help him.

That left only one immediate hope for survival, the lottery ticket. He thought again about redeeming it. It would be suicide to claim the money himself. What he needed was a straw man, a third person above suspicion who could claim it, then give him the money. But there was no one he trusted enough to do it.

****

Bob Hackman watched the news from a hotel room in Santa Barbara, his custom every night when he wasn't working. He saw the Garcia story, growing more worried as the reporter droned on about a murder investigation. If the cops had probable cause to search his house, it looked like his partner might be in serious difficulty. Until now, he wasn't aware Garcia even had a sister and a murder investigation was alarming. People in difficulty with the law often bargained to trade information for a lighter sentence.

The police would be very interested in what his partner knew about him. He could throw away the burner phone used to communicate with Garcia, then disappear. The cops would have no way to find him. But Art could tell them about Teddy Bear Fantasies and help the cops make a sketch of his face. That would endanger the entire operation.

Pulling out his phone, he made a call.

Chapter Twenty-Three

January 21st

After the search of his home, Garcia laid low for a day. The reporters did not go away immediately, but by the next morning he was old news and the vans disappeared. He spent the day sitting in his rocker and getting high, listening to the crows call each other, trying to figure out how he was going to survive. He concluded that he had two choices.

Option one. Get out there and deal drugs to the masses. With luck he'd make enough to pay the mortgage. He would have to take extra precautions to make sure no one followed him. Those detectives had him on their radar, looking for any reason to arrest him.

Option two. Shut it all down, live like a monk inside the house until he lost it through foreclosure, then in his van until he could sell Angela's property. That money would carry him for a while, but what then? Back to dealing?

Neither of these choices would be available if the cops found any kids' fingerprints from the van that could be connected to a name. After being arrested, his new home would be the Atascadero State Prison for many years.

He thought longingly of the lotto ticket. The ticket was his way out of this, and he couldn't cash it, couldn't even tell anybody he had it. Over one hundred million dollars, sitting there waiting for someone to claim it. There must be a solution, but he couldn't think of it.

Dealing was all he had, so he would have to trust in fate. If the police came to arrest him, he would go out like a man. He would rather be dead than rot in a cell for years. After making some calls, he loaded up his car with what he needed, and waited for dark.

When the moon rose, and the crickets sang all around him, he walked down the hill to make sure the reporters had left. Satisfied, he backed his car out of the garage and drove down to the road. He stopped to empty his overflowing mailbox, throwing the mail on his front seat to open later.

Near dawn, Garcia dragged himself home after a long night hustling drugs. He spent half the night reassuring his wealthy clients he had nothing to do with his sister's death. The cops were trying to make him the fall guy but found nothing when they searched his house. The other half he spent selling to the crack heads and tweekers who roamed the streets.

Thanks to the parasite reporter who broadcast to the world the street he lived on, his customers now had a pretty good idea where he lived. There were only a few houses on his street, which was in a rural area. He recalled the warning his mentor gave him years ago when he started selling drugs: *Tell no one where you live. Those crack heads will find you and kill you in your sleep.* He had spent a large sum of money on security to fortify his home, but he wasn't safe there any longer. As soon as possible, he would have to move. His bad luck just kept on coming.

He was in a foul mood when he sorted his mail. One

bulky letter caught his eye, from Scott Alvarez, Attorney at Law. The letter informed him that Alvarez was appointed by Angela Garcia as the executor of her estate. It was his duty to notify all beneficiaries of this and to distribute her assets as instructed. A copy of her will was enclosed.

Art felt a little better. Finally, he'd know once and for all how much he'd get out of Angela. Maybe he could survive after all. He lit another joint and settled down to read the will.

****

Crushed by the news of her lover's murder, Stonehead kept her wits about her during her interview with the detectives. The question about the kid, right at the end of the interview, had been designed to panic her into saying something stupid. Her legal training had saved her. Shut up and leave, just as she had been taught in law school.

The murder made no sense unless Angela was the victim of a random attack. Someone might have tried to rob her. But who knew she had any money in the house? Who else had a motive for murder? She had no enemies. She just floated along on the tide of life. That left only one person, Art Garcia. It was possible he found out about her side business and killed her when she wouldn't give him a cut. Or he thought he would inherit the property if she died. Maybe he found out she didn't leave him the house in her will and killed her in revenge. It was all speculation. She had never met him, and he might be the nicest guy in the world.

A loose end bothered her. The female cop asked why Angela had a kid with her the night she died. Angie had not told her anything about a kid, so something else must have been going on. Who was this kid, why was he there, and what happened to him?

One possibility was Art might have gone to her house that night to pick up the kid and then something happened which led to murder. That meant he was in business with Angela, too. But why would she want to include him? It made little sense.

Had Angie told him about their arrangement? If she did, Stonehead was no longer safe. If they arrested him, he could trade information about her for a lighter sentence. But if she hadn't told her about working with Art, her logical mind whispered, maybe she hadn't told her brother about her either. A high stakes game of poker was being played out, and Stonehead didn't know who had the winning hand.

Arriving home from work that evening, she checked her mailbox on the way to her front door. There were a few letters, which she sorted through. One letter, from Scott Alvarez, Attorney at Law, looked important. Opening the envelope, she found a letter announcing his appointment as executor of Angela's estate, as well as a copy of her will.

The letter stated that all beneficiaries were being notified. Therefore, Garcia must have received a copy of the will, too. So now he knew he wasn't inheriting Angela's property. Stonehead felt uneasy about that. It was only natural that he would want to know why a perfect stranger was the primary beneficiary of his sister's estate instead of him, and she was the only one who could tell him the answer.

It would be best if they never met.

Chapter Twenty-Four

June 2016

Outside the courtroom of the Honorable John Hidy, Angela sat on a bench covered in graffiti, waiting for her case to be called. She'd been assigned a one-day-old baby girl, abandoned in a trash bin a month ago. After a sanitation worker heard the baby crying and called 9-1-1, she was rushed to the hospital where a routine blood sample detected heroin.

The police found nothing with the baby that would identify the parents. Unable to get any additional information from canvassing the neighborhood, they handed the case off to Child Services.

Aided by the frequent retirements of senior personnel above her, Angela now held the number two position in her office. She dealt with the lowest forms of humanity: parents so damaged by drugs or their own crappy childhoods their own children meant nothing to them. The older kids were the worst, abused for so long many were beyond saving without expensive psychological counseling and a stable home—things the county could not supply.

There was no room in her heart for pity. Her childhood had been shitty too, but she rose above it to make something of herself. No reason these kids couldn't do the same, but they were lazy, and didn't try.

Instead, the county was forced to take care of them until they reached the age of eighteen.

She was reviewing this latest Baby Jane Doe file, formulating a recommendation to the court, when someone sat down on the bench next to her. The person sat uncomfortably close, causing her to look up in annoyance. Patsy Stonehead, one of the bottom feeders of the county court system, smiled at her. They had tried many cases together over the years; Angela felt Patsy was the most competent of the bunch.

All the lawyers appointed by the court to defend the parents and their kids were known as bottom feeders. She was contemptuous of them. Most had trouble passing the bar exam, ran afoul of the state bar ethics rules, or had drug problems of their own. The county paid them a small fee for each case. This was how they survived, doing the bare minimum necessary to represent their clients.

Stonehead was a tall blonde, with an attractive body and well-styled hair that smelled of lavender. Dressing better than most of the bottom feeders, she wore a gray wool skirt with a matching jacket. Under the jacket was a ruffled black silk blouse. A pair of expensive black leather pumps highlighted her tan legs.

Because she didn't like being physically close to anyone, Angela shifted over on the bench to reestablish her personal space. "How you doing, Patsy?"

"Good. Got two hearings in front of Judge Franklin today. I heard you got the trash can baby case."

"Another tragedy," she said, with no emotion.

A large noisy family walked by, herded by their lawyer toward a courtroom.

"Do you get many of these abandoned baby cases?"

"More than I want," Angie replied, wondering why she cared.

Patsy's gaze darted around the hall, making sure no one could hear her. "It seems a shame to waste so much court time on these cases. Don't all these babies end up getting adopted out to somebody?"

"What's your point?"

A lawyer jogged by, late for a hearing, looking worried.

She lowered her voice. "Do you know some people pay big money for a baby? They can't have kids of their own, but they don't want to wait in line forever to adopt like everyone else?"

"Yeah, private adoptions. We don't get involved with those," Angela said dismissively.

"Suppose there was a way for a kid like this trash can baby to have that happen? Somebody might pay quite a bit of money to adopt her," Patsy replied with a sideways glance.

Angela looked at her, not understanding. "What are you saying? She needs papers for that. We don't have a clue who her parents are. It would never pass muster with the court."

She was nodding her head. "All true, but what if there were ways, hypothetically, to create the paperwork, make up a birth certificate, and get the kid adopted out of state?"

Speechless, Angela put down the case file and just stared at her.

Patsy checked her watch. "Shit, I'm due in court. Why don't we meet after work privately and talk? Call me, here's my card." Pressing it into her hand, she smiled and walked away, melting into the crowd.

The conversation surprised yet somehow intrigued Angela. The more she thought about it, the more sense it made. Give these babies to someone who wanted them, save the county the cost of care, and make some money for herself. It looked like a win for everyone involved.

Did Patsy have the connections to create the fake documents to support a private adoption? Was that her game, to find adoptable babies and ship them out of state? It would take a large bunch of crooked lawyers to make that happen. An entire network of people willing to not ask questions. It seemed to be impossible.

The court bailiff stuck his head out the door. "Judge Hidy's ready for you now."

Gathering up her paperwork, she trudged into the courtroom, demoralized and burned out. She would spend the next several months grinding through the bureaucracy to get the trash can baby on the road to adoption. And nobody would care.

Chapter Twenty-Five

Later that night, at home in her sweltering converted garage, Angela took Patsy's card out of her purse. She stared at it, trying to decide whether to take the next step. There was an enormous amount of risk if she got involved, such as picking the right babies with no family ties, then intervening in the usual process before the County created any records. On top of that, she'd have to figure out a way to gain physical custody of the baby and keep it hidden until it could be passed off. So much could go wrong.

On the other hand, it was impossible to achieve the comfortable life she dreamed of on the salary the County paid. She wanted to own a house, have nice clothes, and take lavish vacations like the rich and famous. The reality was she lived from paycheck to paycheck, with little left over at the end of the month.

Weighing the pros and cons in her mind, she finally decided it wouldn't hurt to talk further. She dialed Patsy's number.

The meeting was set for next day after work, at a small park in the foothills above Santa Barbara. It was an ideal location. There was only one road that led there. And from the overlook at the park, the traffic coming up the road was easy to monitor.

After leaving work, Angela pointed her car up the hill. There was no one else on the road. As she drove higher into the foothills, still not seeing any other cars, she got an uneasy feeling she was being set up. Maybe Patsy worked for the Feds, trying to entrap people working for Child Services. So far, no laws had been broken, so if she blew off the meeting, she would be safe.

She was looking for a place to turn her car around on the narrow road when the park came into view. The parking lot contained only one car. Somewhat reassured, she slowly turned into the lot, ready to flee at the first sign of danger. Patsy waved from the overlook.

After parking the car, Angela walked to her. "Spying on me?" she asked, with a nod for the binoculars in her hand.

"Just making sure nobody followed you."

This annoyed her. "Look, you contacted me, remember? I came to hear what you have to say, not get you busted."

Patsy smiled through tightly pressed lips. "I'm paranoid about security. This is a very risky business and I have to be careful. I need to ask you for one more favor before we talk."

"What is it?"

"To pat you down, just to make sure nobody is listening. To be fair, you can do the same to me. Then we can talk, okay?"

Angela's first reaction was to say no. Being asked to allow a stranger to grope her was an invasion of personal space, which she never allowed. But another part of her brain said Patsy was a woman, and therefore the rules were different. Hesitating, she reached a compromise. Holding both hands out at her sides, she closed her eyes.

When the pat down began, she was surprised at her reaction. It felt… good. She didn't know why. When

Patsy cupped her breasts, massaging them briefly before moving on down her legs, she wanted to ask her to do it again.

Angela's heart pounded. A new emotion was present...what was it....desire? The realization hit her like a sledgehammer. Was she gay? The answer to why she never felt attracted to men? She opened her eyes as her friend finished and stepped back.

"Now it's your turn," Patsy said with an inviting smile as she held out her hands from her sides.

Petrified, Angela froze. How could she do this? What if she was wrong and wasn't gay? What if she offended her friend? A primal drive inside her brain threw all this aside and drove her forward. She *needed* to do this. Copying the process, she ran her hands down Patsy's back and sides. Then she cupped her breasts and massaged them. Patsy gave a soft groan and leaned in. The lavender scent was still in her hair.

Now mere inches apart, they stared hungrily into each other's eyes. Coming together with a light kiss, emotions exploded. There was no doubt left in Angela's mind, she liked women. They broke away from each other, afraid to go any further in public view.

Patsy's voice came out in a breathless squeak. "I didn't know you were gay."

Angie was trying to come to grips with it. There was the possibility of a relationship...but what to do...suppose she made a fool of herself? The best way forward, she decided, was to be honest. "I didn't know either. I...I've never felt like this."

"Not until now?"

Embarrassed, she ducked her head down. "No."

Patsy looked like she wanted to cry. Stepping

forward, she enveloped her friend in a fierce hug. "We have a lot to talk about besides business. Why don't we go to my place where there is a little more privacy?"

Angela hesitated. This was it…the moment of truth…there would be no going back if she agreed, but it all seemed so right. "Let's go."

****

Her host made a pitcher of martinis and showed her the view from the deck attached to the master bedroom. The mountains looming in the distance in the twilight were enhanced by the smell of the night blooming jasmine in the backyard. An owl glided by, silently searching for dinner. They made small talk while sipping on their drinks.

"This is a beautiful house," Angela said. "Have you lived here long?"

Patsy laughed. "Until two years ago I couldn't afford to buy anything in Santa Barbara."

"I totally get that. I'm living in a shithole converted garage, barely able to afford the rent. Santa Barbara is a wonderful place to live if you're rich. Otherwise it sucks."

"Here's to you getting rich." Raising her glass, Angela did the same. A soft clink as the glasses touched was followed by sips of the liquor.

The pitcher of margaritas disappeared. The alcohol did its job to break the tension and loosen inhibitions. It was a short stroll back into the bedroom.

When it was over, Angela wanted nothing more than to stay there forever, exploring a lifestyle which she never imagined existed for her. Life had a new meaning; feelings of love for someone who would love her back. She was unbelievably happy.

"Wow," she said, overwhelmed by it all. "I've missed so much and lost so much time I can never get back. You opened my eyes to who I am. I was stumbling around like a blind woman and didn't know it."

Patsy turned to face her. "I'm sorry it took you so long to find yourself. It's not a simple thing to do; it goes against everything they teach you growing up. I was lucky; I knew I was gay in high school. Since then, I've lived my life without pretending. Society is more accepting of gay people now; we don't have to hide it."

"Will you teach me?"

"Of course I will. There's an entire community of lesbians in Santa Barbara you should meet. There are others out there, women you might enjoy being with even more than me!"

"I'll love no one more than you."

She smiled. "We'll see about that."

Chapter Twenty-Six

The following day, when five o'clock finally rolled around, Angela drove straight to her lover's house. They'd made arrangements to continue the discussion of baby adoptions, which they never quite got around to the previous night. She wasn't sure how to act. Falling in love overrode all the whispering in her brain, telling her this baby thing was an insane idea. But did her friend feel the same way? Had yesterday been a onetime event or the beginning of something deeper between them?

Patsy put her fears to rest quickly, enveloping her in her arms as soon as the door closed. Their lips touched, tentatively at first, then with increasing passion. Hands explored each other's bodies, whispers of love between them, and Angela knew the relationship was real. For the first time in her life, she felt loved. There was no longer any question in her mind. She would do whatever Patsy wanted her to do.

After several minutes of foreplay, Patsy reluctantly pulled away. "We'd better cut this out or we'll be spending all night up in the bedroom again instead of talking about business. Come on, I'm making dinner."

Angela followed her down the hallway to the kitchen. She sat on a barstool, leaning on a counter that separated the kitchen from the dining room. A martini waited for her there. The conversation began.

"How did you get into this baby thing?"

"A lawyer friend recruited me two years ago when I was having a hard time making a living here. The company, Parent Connections, specializes in finding babies for wealthy people who don't want to wait years to adopt through the normal processes."

"How do they get away with it?"

"They tell the clients a teenage girl in another state gave birth and agreed to put the baby up for private adoption. In return for the baby, the client pays a fee, which they are told covers the mother's medical expenses, schooling, and other things. The company creates a set of papers, making everything look legal. They have excellent forgers. Clients must sign an agreement prohibiting them from telling anyone where the baby came from and agreeing not to attempt contact the mother."

"How much will they pay?"

"The fee varies by what the company feels the client will pay. They guarantee at least twenty-five thousand dollars for each healthy baby you deliver to them."

All this sounded good to Angela. She had one stipulation, that her identity remain secret. Her new partner agreed it was a good idea so no one could attempt to blackmail her.

"How hard will it be for you to get a baby?"

"It may take a while," Angela admitted. "I can only take one that has no parents and no possibility of anyone else ever looking for it. Once I find one, I'll make sure the baby never gets input into our computer system. The county will never know the baby exists. Then it gets easy. All I have to do is deliver it to you."

****

Two weeks later, Angela received a call from Beth

Logan, her contact at the hospital. The police had found a baby girl tucked into a soiled blanket next to her dead mother in an abandoned building on the outskirts of downtown. They found no identification on the mother or daughter, but DNA results proved the connection. Efforts to locate witnesses to provide information proved fruitless.

The baby was taken to the hospital for a routine physical exam, which found her to be malnourished but otherwise healthy, with no trace of drugs in her system. Now the hospital was ready to discharge her to Child Services.

The baby fit all the criteria. It was time for action.

"Beth," Angela said, "I'm sending over a caseworker by the name of Christine Ravine to collect the baby. She'll be there late afternoon sometime."

"If she isn't here before I get off work, tell her to ask for Austin Study."

"Will do."

Angela left the office after telling her boss she needed a few hours off to take care of some personal things, and drove to Patsy's home, to which she now had a key. The next step was to change into her disguise. Donning a blonde wig, she lightened the color of her face and hands with makeup. Next, she changed into a pants suit she would dispose of once she handed off the baby. A precaution in case surveillance cameras at the hospital recorded her movements. She slipped on a pair of tennis shoes, handy if she needed to run from the hospital. To complete the disguise, an enormous pair of dark sunglasses hid her face.

She appraised herself in the bathroom mirror. Would the disguise protect her from being recognized?

There was no way to be sure except by walking into the place. Many people working there knew her. This was the point where she took the most risk. A single person recognizing her would ruin the plan and send her to jail.

The tension kept building, causing her shoulders to ache. *Last chance to abort the mission,* she thought. Taking a shaky breath, she grabbed her purse, and headed for the door.

Chapter Twenty-Seven

Mercy Hospital in Santa Barbara was a very busy place. Located west of the 101 freeway in an otherwise residential neighborhood, it dominated the area. Angela came here occasionally to pick up an abandoned child, coordinating things with Beth Logan, who would recognize her even in disguise. But Beth got off work at four p.m. and Angela had never met Austin Study, the guy who worked swing shift, so her visit was planned for late afternoon.

At four thirty, she entered through the automatic sliding doors and stopped at the information desk in the lobby. "I'm meeting Austin Study, to take custody of a baby. Let him know I'm here," she ordered the candy striper, hoping to intimidate her into not asking questions.

"Uh, okay," she said after glancing at Christine's ID. She dialed Study's extension. "I've got a woman at reception from Child Services, here to pick up a baby."

"Send her back, room one twenty."

After being provided a visitor's badge and directions, Angela entered the main hospital. She wandered the labyrinth of halls, keeping her head down, peering at numbers on the doors, until she found room one twenty. She took a deep breath to settle her nerves. Several people, whom she knew, passed her in the hall with little more than a passing glance.

Her disguise was working.

Study was sitting behind a large metal desk when she knocked and entered. Piles of paper covered the desk. Three five drawer file cabinets stood like soldiers along the back wall. Two straight-back chairs took up the remaining space. It was a small room, and no one else was there. He rose, extending his hand. "Hi, I'm Austin Study."

Angela noticed his perfect white teeth. His face was round and tanned. A pair of rectangular eyeglasses framed brown eyes. "Christine Ravine from Child Services. I'm here to pick up an abandoned baby."

"Beth told me you would come. I haven't met you before. Are you new?"

"I was hired a few months ago so I'm still learning the job."

"It's pretty simple. We fill out the paperwork, and I give you the baby. Won't take very long," he assured her. "Please have a seat."

She sat down and waited while he yanked open a drawer in his desk and removed a stack of papers. "Ready to go. First thing is I need to see is your ID,"

Angela reached into her purse and removed her fake Child Services ID. He took it, copying her employee number onto the form, made a photocopy, and gave it back to her. If anyone ever checked, they would not find an employee with that name and ID number working for the county. No one could trace her that way.

The next half hour was devoted to signing documents whereby Child Services acknowledged they were taking sole custody of an abandoned baby girl. The girl was known as Jane Doe 19/16. The19 indicated she was the 19th unknown baby taken to the hospital that year. The 16 was for the year, 2016. Angela wondered how many of those nineteen babies she could have taken if she had partnered with Patsy earlier. A stack of several hundred thousand dollars could be in her safe, and the county saved of much expense. She sighed. It didn't matter now.

"Sorry this is taking so long," Study apologized, mistaking her sigh as a sign of impatience. "You know how the government works."

"Oh, I'm fine with it," Angela said, not wanting to deflect his attention from the paperwork. "Just thinking of all the things I need to do tonight. There's never enough time."

Study redoubled his efforts and ten minutes later she signed the last document. "That's it," he declared. "We can go get the baby now."

They walked down a noisy, crowded corridor to a bank of elevators. Pediatrics was on the second floor. She put on her sunglasses, telling him the florescent lighting hurt her eyes. Her real concern was running into somebody who might recognize her.

When the elevator doors opened onto the second floor, they made a right turn, following the signs to pediatrics. A glassed-in wall, the viewing area for the nursery, signaled their arrival. Study marched past the glass to a security door with a keypad on it and punched in several numbers. A soft buzz and the door unlocked, allowing them to enter a small room. The only way out was through a second door with another keypad lock, to which he did not know the combination. An intercom hung on the wall to his right, and a security camera angled down from the ceiling. Angela avoided looking at it. They were in a mantrap, unable to proceed until buzzed in by someone on the inside. After he pressed the button on the intercom, it squawked to life and a disembodied voice asked, *"Hi, Austin. Are you here for the baby?"*

"Yep. Got Christine from Child Services with me."

"I'll let you in."

The second door buzzed, and the two of them moved into the inner sanctum. The sound of crying babies filled the air. Directly in front of them was the nursing station, manned by two women dressed in hospital scrubs. Angela didn't recognize either of them.

"How's it going, Sherry?" Study asked with a smile.

"Fair to middling," she replied with a weary grin. "We've got a full house. Glad one is leaving."

He chuckled. Angela gave her a sly smile but said nothing.

"Let's move that baby out of here," he said.

He introduced Christine, who nodded and shook hands. Handing the paperwork to Sherry, he waited patiently while she reviewed it and put it into the baby's file. "I'll go get her," she said.

She disappeared through a door leading into the nursery. In five minutes she was back with Jane Doe 19/16, wrapped up snugly in a pink blanket. She handed the baby to Angela, who made the appropriate comments about her beauty. In reality, she had no feelings at all toward the baby. She was cargo, to be transported to the buyers as soon as possible.

Sherry strode back into the nursery, returning with a plastic bag containing diapers, baby powder, and other freebies the hospital gave every new parent. She handed the bag to Angela.

"I guess that's it," said Study. "See ya soon."

They reentered the mantrap. The first door closed, and the second door buzzed, letting them out into the hallway. Fighting an urge to run as fast as she could, she strolled back to the elevator.

"Shouldn't be hard to get this one adopted," Study noted.

If you only knew, she thought. A white baby girl, in good health, would be very much in demand.

"Be months before the court settles anything," she replied, trying to sound weary.

The elevator stopped, and the door opened. They both stepped out into the usual bedlam that goes on in a busy hospital. It was time to get out of here, while her luck still held. The longer she stayed, the greater the chance of being recognized.

"I need to get going. It's getting late, and I must deliver her to foster care. Thanks so much for your help." Angela gave him a smile, hoping he would find it flattering.

"I understand," he replied. "Do you need any help loading up the baby?"

"No, I'm good. I've got the car seat ready to go. Thanks!"

She shifted the baby to her left arm so she could shake hands. At the lobby, she dropped off her visitor's badge. Exiting the way she entered, she strode to her car, keeping her head down. The closer she got to it, the more the tension built. She imagined the sounds of running footsteps behind her, and her heart pounded.

The baby made short, squeaky noises, looking at her new environment with wide eyes while Angela wrestled with the car seat. Drenched in sweat and hyperventilating, she felt exhilarated. Everything went according to plan. She was a ghost that existed only on her ID badge.

If the hospital suspected anything, Child Services would get an inquiry, which the District Supervisor would refer to her to handle. The early warning would give her valuable time to pack up and disappear before the authorities realized who they were dealing with. The plan seemed foolproof.

She glanced over her shoulder at the baby now asleep in the backseat and smiled. Jane Doe 19/16 was money in the bank.

****

The next two days were agonizing. Angela expected the cops to show up and arrest her any minute. The handoff of the baby to Patsy went smoothly, but a nagging feeling she forgot something plagued her. Certain she covered her tracks…no one was searching for the baby…but fate sometimes intervened in the best laid plans.

If somebody recognized her, she would be finished, in jail for a long time…but what did she *forget*…should she get ready to flee…where would she go? The questions kept repeating themselves over and over in her mind, driving her crazy. Even her boss asked if something was wrong.

The morning of the third day, she was at her desk writing up another of the endless reports when her cell phone rang. "Hello?"

"Hi back at ya," Patsy replied.

This was the code they had agreed on to signal everything went as planned.

"Thank God. Are you back?"

"I got in an hour ago. See you tonight."

Tension drained from her body. "Okay, bye,"

At five o'clock, she grabbed her purse and rushed out of the office, driving straight to her lover's house. Patsy opened the door with a huge grin on her face and a glass of wine in her hand. She was wearing an old pink terrycloth bathrobe and a pair of worn slippers. Standing aside, she allowed Angela to enter, shutting the door behind her. The two of them embraced, dancing around and laughing.

Patsy gasped for air. "Wait…wait! You've got to see this!" she cried, taking her partner's hand and guiding her upstairs to the master bedroom. She pointed to a duffel bag on the bed.

Angela zipped it open and saw money, more than she had ever seen in one place in her life, all stacked in bundles of hundred-dollar bills banded together. Fifteen bundles, each one containing two thousand dollars, sat in the bag. She did the math in her head. Thirty thousand dollars.

"Wow," she said, still finding it hard to believe the whole thing had gone so smoothly.

"It's all yours, babe. The company gave you a bonus of five thousand for the right baby. And I've got another bonus for you right here."

Patsy let her bathrobe fall to the floor. She wore nothing but a smile and her signature scent.

Chapter Twenty-Eight

September 2016

Angela went back to work, waiting for an opportunity to steal another baby. She had to be picky, which proved to be a problem. By the end of summer, she took only two more. After three months, she had eighty thousand dollars stashed away in her safe, but she wasn't satisfied. This amount wouldn't begin to satisfy her goals.

There were older children who occasionally fit the criteria to disappear, but Parent Connections wanted only babies. Their wealthy clientele were not interested in adopting older children. Angela felt like she was missing an opportunity. The solution was to find another client willing to take the older children and pay well. The problem was finding one. Though stymied, she kept trying to think of a way to make it work.

In the middle of September, she responded to a police request to pick up a child at an abandoned warehouse on Fleet Street. The whole area was filthy. Graffiti covered the walls of the abandoned buildings. Roads in and out were dotted with potholes. Trash filled the gutters and blew down the sidewalks. The smell of rotting garbage filled the air. A very thin stray dog slunk away across the street.

At the corner of the block, a small knot of people

stood in a circle. To her trained eye, it looked like a drug deal. A muscular man with his back to her was exchanging something for money from a derelict. The man seemed familiar. As she moved closer to the corner, a ragged druggie in the group jerked his head up, saw her coming, and spoke to the muscular man.

Straightening, the man glanced quickly over his shoulder in her direction. He said a few words to the group and disappeared around the corner. Angela stopped walking, confused by what she saw. She got only a glimpse of the man's face, but it was her brother.

****

That night, home alone, she thought about possibilities. Art was a fuckup, incapable of getting, then keeping, a well-paying job. His track record since graduating from high school proved that. He had no job skills for which anyone would pay him well, which explained why he had lived at home his whole life. But the last time they talked, he had mentioned having a new job and getting an apartment. Dealing drugs was a career opportunity open to anyone, particularly those with no skills.

Rather than being upset that her brother was a drug dealer, Angela saw an opportunity. A dealer would know other criminals involved in the trade. Maybe those criminals did other things besides selling drugs. Perhaps they would be interested in the adoption business.

The following day, during lunch break, she called Art from her car, where no one could overhear the conversation.

"What's up Angie?"

"Just another wonderful day dealing with unfit parents and wasted kids."

"They ought to sterilize all them assholes. They got no business havin' kids."

"Yeah, there're way too many kids out there the County has to support with our taxes. The entire system is rotten. Listen," she said, changing the subject, "I was wondering about your new job. Sorry I didn't ask about it last time we spoke. How's that goin' for you?"

"All good. Still settlin' in," he replied vaguely.

"I'm proud of you. I'm sure it sucked living with Dad for so long. So what are you doing?" She tapped her fingers on the steering wheel, impatient with the lack of information.

"What the hell, Angie. We don't talk for years, now you need to know my whole life?" he shot back.

He's doing something illegal, or he'd be bragging about it, she thought. Time to move on with the plan.

"Sorry, bro. No offense, just trying to catch up with things. It doesn't matter to me what you do. Believe me; I've seen the worst of humanity in my job. Got to do whatever it takes to make a living, right?"

"That's right. But some things are better kept private. Shit, you're more private than me. I don't even know where your crib is!"

She realized he was right. "Guess we're even then. I don't have any idea where you live either. Me, I'm living in a shithole converted garage, which is embarrassing. Don't want anybody to see it. What's your excuse?"

He was unsure how much to share with her. "Nobody knows where I live, Angie. All I can say is its better for ever 'body that way. Got to trust me on that."

His answer confirmed her suspicions enough to get to the point of her call. "Art, I've been doing some thinking. I've got an idea that might make us both some serious money, if you're interested…" she let her voice trail off.

"Okay, Angie. I got shit to attend to, so say what you got to say so I can get on with it," he said impatiently.

"All right, I'm laying all my cards on the table, no bullshit. Just listen to what I have to say, and then you get your turn. Okay?" She didn't wait for a reply. "Like I said, I'm not making any judgments about your business. If you're doin' good, I'm happy for you. But I could make both of us a lot of money if you can help me make some connections. To do that, you need to know the right people. Not your law-abiding types, understand?" She paused, waiting for some signal that he was interested.

"Yeah, I get it," Art answered, curiosity in his voice.

She was reeling him in. "So here's what I know. You're dealing drugs."

There was silence on the line, so she continued. "You were dealing over on Fleet Street when I was out on a case. I saw your face when you glanced over your shoulder. You're real secretive about your job and where you live, which is not like you. So, like I said, if this is something you're doing, I'm okay with it; you can help me with my problem of finding the right people to talk to. If I'm all wrong, there's no point in talking any more about this." She had baited the hook.

There was still silence on the line. Angela waited patiently. "I might have some connections, 'pends on what you lookin' for," he said grudgingly.

So far, everything was going well. Now came the moment of truth. It was necessary to take a risk, laying out her plan, not knowing if he could help her or not. If he couldn't, she would be telling him way too much incriminating information he could use against her. She didn't like that. But this was her best chance to find the people she needed, and greed goaded her on.

"Here's my idea. Right now, it's just an idea. You might think it's crazy, but I've thought about it a lot, and I think with the right circumstances it could work."

Angela would not mention she was already stealing babies. He didn't need to know about that. Reclining her car seat, she got a little more comfortable, and began.

"In my job, I deal with kids all the time. Some of them are abandoned or their parents are dead, and there's no next of kin we can find. These kids end up as wards of the court and spend time in foster homes until they get adopted or turn eighteen. They're messed up when I get them, and foster homes make them worse."

"Here's my idea. Suppose one of these abandoned kids was made available for adoption to the highest bidder, somebody who doesn't want to wait in line to adopt, and we split the money? I supply the kid; you supply the connections to the buyer and deliver the kid. Do you know the right people who could help with that?"

"Angie," he replied. "Why you want to take that big a risk? If you get busted, you goin' away for a long time."

"I've thought about all that. It's not as risky as you think. All kinds of records can disappear with my full access to the database. My job is to get the kid to a safe place where you can pick it up. Then you deliver it to your contact that day, and we're done. We can get at least thirty thousand for the right kid. If I get caught, we'll set it up so nobody is going to be suspecting you. Your only risk is getting busted while transporting the kid."

"But why you need to do this, Angie? You got a genuine job, not like me. Are you in trouble?"

"No trouble." She hesitated, not wanting to disclose her personal motivation but realizing he needed more convincing.

"I…I need a better life. The county pays me just enough to survive. I can't afford anything nice like a house, vacations, stuff like that. You can relate to that, right? It's not fair. All these rich people are living the good life around here, and I want a piece of that myself. After the life I've had, I deserve it. These kids…they're in bad shape, Art…and the county doesn't care. Let them go to somebody who might help. What's wrong with us making some money doing that?"

"Nothin' wrong with it, Angie. I just got to understand it, that's all. The money sounds good, but you can't spend it in jail. Tell me the details, how it works, from the beginnin'."

She laid it all out for him, without mentioning she already did this with Patsy. He listened, interrupting every so often to clarify a point. When she finished, he was silent, thinking it over.

"I see how this could work. But I got to ask 'round, see if anybody is into this. Wouldn't be the same people I'm workin' with now, understand?"

"Okay, I get it. Just one thing…don't tell anybody where these kids are coming from, okay? I don't want to have anything to do with them."

"Sure, Angie that goes without sayin'. You know I'm solid." He paused. "This may take a while. I got to be careful who I talk with. Not too many locals 'round with the *cajones* to handle somethin' this heavy. I'll call you when somethin' pops."

"That's fine. Let's not talk about kids on the phone. Let's call them something else…um…how about a package? That way, if anybody is listening, it's just a normal conversation, okay?"

"Good idea. Got to be careful, sis. This ain't no game we're playin' here."

Chapter Twenty-Nine

January 22nd

Ron strode through the back door at the station, trading insults with the other cops while making his way to his desk. It was Monday, and everyone was in a good mood after a few days off. Being able to sleep in his own bed did wonders for his disposition.

It came as a surprise when he found Mary Ann's desk unoccupied. This was one of maybe five times he beat her into work since they became partners. Picking up his coffee cup, he kept on moving toward the break room, drawn by the aroma of brewing coffee.

There, he found Warner eying the coffee pot with suspicion. "Don't know if my stomach can take any more coffee today."

"I hear you, LT. When was the last time somebody cleaned that thing out?"

"1999, I think. The chief was holding a staff meeting here, and heard the coffee was lethal so he made sure the staff cleaned the coffee pot out before the meeting." He glanced around the crowded break room, then said under his breath, "Come to my office. We need to talk."

Ron filled his cup and followed him back to his office.

"Shut the door," the Lieutenant said as he settled into his chair. "Any progress on the Garcia case?"

Ron filled him in on the search of the house and the feeling he had about the fingerprints in the van.

"So you think Garcia was at the house and killed Angela over this kid? And then took him somewhere?" Warner asked.

"That's one possibility," Ron said. "I don't know if the kid is connected to the murder or if the two are separate things. But I've got a gut feeling this kid is the key to the entire case. All I've got right now is the word of the neighbor who said she saw a kid there. The kid just disappeared, and I can't figure out what happened to him. I think Stonehead is part of this too, but I've got no proof she and Garcia even know each other."

"The search warrant didn't turn up anything but Garcia's pistol, so I think he was expecting us and got rid of everything. Forensics did find some kids prints in his van. I'm chasing that down. I need to call facilities again and see what the holdup is to getting a locksmith out here to open the safe and see if there's anything in there that can help us."

"Have you checked missing persons for any kids?"

"We did; we got zip."

The lieutenant scratched his head. "I have to ask myself where Angela would get a kid that nobody is looking for. She'd dealt with a lot of them through Child Services, didn't she?"

"Yeah, but we've been told the kids are all tracked from the time they get picked up. So if one disappeared, there would be a record, and somebody would start asking questions. Nobody has any kids unaccounted for. So if she took this kid, she did it some other way. If we had a name, we could trace it back, maybe find out why he's not in the computer."

"Then again," Ron said, "if the kid came from somewhere else, we might be going down the wrong trail. It could have been a kidnapping for ransom, and the parents were warned not to call the police. Or perhaps the kid has nothing to do with the case. Angela might have been babysitting that day and the parents came by and picked him up before she died. I'm praying we get a match on the prints."

"All right, keep it moving," Warner ordered. "The media are all over this now and calling me daily for answers."

Ron took his coffee back to his desk. Mary Ann was there, pecking away on her keyboard. She looked haggard.

"Nice to see you, partner."

Looking up, she stopped typing. "Tomas caught something and kept me up all night. I couldn't get him to go to sleep. How can a baby cry for hours?"

Shrugging, he sat down at his desk. He was the wrong person to be talking to about kids. He made a call to facilities, complaining about the lack of progress in getting a locksmith to open the safe. No one was available until the 24th.

Seething with frustration, he turned to his partner. "We can't get the safe open until the 24th because the damn locksmith is on vacation. The geniuses in management don't have anybody else approved to work on it."

"Crap," said Mary Ann. "I'm going to be retired before we solve this case. We need to get ballistics to test Garcia's pistol, see if it fired the bullet that killed Angela. If they match, we can arrest him right now."

Ron nodded. "I'll send the pistol over this morning.

The weakest link in the case is Stonehead. We've got nothing to prove she knows Art or anything about the kid. We need to find something else to tie her into this. Sheila's going to subpoena her bank statements for the last year, so we can see if she's been making any unusual deposits."

"We've still got to confirm she was talking to her mother around the time of death," Mary Ann reminded him. "She gave us permission to access her call records."

Ron's frustration grew by increments. "Something has to break this open. Let's go visit the Garcias' aunt, Rosa Hernandez, and see if she can tell us anything. We can't do much else until the prints come back."

Chapter Thirty

The administrator of the Sunrise Assisted Living Facility accompanied the detectives to Rosa Hernandez's room. "These two people are from the police department. They want to talk to you about your niece, Angela," she said when they stood in the doorway.

Ron peered past her at the only occupant in the room. She was a petite woman, lost in an oversized recliner chair. A pink house dress covered her tiny frame, black bedroom slippers covered her feet. Thinning gray hair was gathered in a bun in back of her deeply lined face. Her eyes were black as coal as she twisted her head to stare at her visitors.

After Ron and Mary Ann introduced themselves, she waved them to the two visitors' chairs. The cozy room was just large enough to contain a twin bed, an end table with a lamp and alarm clock, three chairs, and a low dresser upon which a flat screen TV showed an old movie. Photographs of various people hung in frames on the walls. A sliding glass door led outside to a small patio.

The administrator said goodbye and left, closing the door behind her. Mary Ann started the conversation. "Mrs. Hernandez, we are investigating the death of Angela Garcia, your niece. Were you aware she is deceased?"

Looking exasperated, she raised both hands, palms

out. "It's been all over the news. How could I not know?"

"Just needed to make sure," Mary Ann replied, embarrassed. "We are gathering information on Angela's life as a child, growing up in Montecito. This information may help us determine who killed her. You are the last of her relatives still alive who knew her well and could help us with this. Can we ask you a few questions?"

Rosa sat still for a moment, her black eyes never leaving the detective. She raised a finger, twisted with arthritis, and shook it at her. "So now you want me to tell you about that poor girl, all the family secrets? Then you will tell those nasty reporters so they can say bad things about her on TV. How's that going to help her? Joe did his best to raise his kids right; it wasn't him that did the damage."

Ron leaned forward. "Mrs. Hernandez, you have my word any information you give us today will remain confidential. We will not share it with anyone outside the police department. Don't you want justice for your niece?"

Rosa turned to stare at him, looking him up and down. After a moment, which seemed an eternity, she cleared her throat and spoke softly. "Of course she deserves justice. It should have happened years ago when she was young and couldn't defend herself. It's too late now."

She gazed out to the patio, lost in thought. Pain was etched on her face. When Ron coughed delicately, her focus went back to him. "I will tell you a story. It was so long ago sometimes I think it never happened. My memory isn't as sharp as it used to be, but something like this you can't forget. Believe me, I've tried."

"Go on, please," Mary Ann urged.

Rosa rearranged her body in the chair before she began speaking again. "Joe's wife, Sara, behaved like a child when he married her. She relied on him for everything. We all warned him something was wrong, but he loved her and wouldn't listen. When she got older, she became more confident and started working. Joe was okay with that until she had the two kids and he wanted her to quit her job and stay home to raise them. That's what women do, isn't it?"

She stopped talking and looked at Ron for approval. He nodded to encourage her to continue.

"By that time, Sara thought her job was more important than raising kids, so Joe had to force her to quit. That's when the trouble started. She drank a lot and blamed the kids for having to quit her job. Without a career, she felt her life had no meaning."

"When Angela came home from school, her mother would beat her. We all saw the bruises, but nobody did anything. Sara would scream at her, tell her she was worthless and regretted she was born. Can you imagine what that does to a kid? I know for a fact she locked Angela in a closet for hours at a time. God only knows what else she did to her.

"That poor child blamed herself, thought she did something wrong by being born. Shut herself off from everyone. I guess it was the only way she knew to keep her sanity. This continued on for years until she went away to college. She shunned the entire family after that. I saw her at her mother's funeral, and she was very cold and calculating. I couldn't get her to talk at all."

"How was her brother treated?" asked Mary Ann.

"Art fared no better. He grew up afraid of

everything, with no confidence at all. Joe didn't know what to do. He tried to help the kids, but my brother loved Sara so much he wouldn't believe she could do things like that."

As Rosa finished her story, she appeared to be even smaller, as though telling the story allowed the guilt to escape her body, leaving a shrunken, broken woman sitting in the chair. She cried silently, her cheeks glistening with tears.

"So now you know the family secrets. You should arrest me. I knew what was going on, but the family said to be quiet, we would work it out ourselves. The police would bring shame to our family name. I could have saved her, and maybe she'd be alive today. I'll take that to my grave. Please put me in jail. I don't belong here."

Ron had a lump in his throat. He didn't know what to say.

Mary Ann broke the silence. "I'm so sorry you had to live with this," she whispered. "It was not your fault. In your culture, women are expected to let the men make the decisions. You are as much a victim as Angela. Joe should have stopped it. All you can do now is try to forgive yourself. God will be your judge, Rosa, not the police."

Mary Ann stood up and bent down to give her a kiss on her forehead. Ron stood nearby until she broke away, then they backed out of the room.

Chapter Thirty-One

"So now we know why Angela didn't like kids," Mary Ann mused. "Whatever she did with or to that kid before she died wasn't good. If we rule out kidnapping as a motive, did she plan to kill him?"

It was late afternoon. The detectives sat at their desks, trying to fit Rosa's story into the investigation. Outside, dark clouds blocked the sun. More rain was on the way.

"That doesn't fit," said Ron. "If she planned to kill him and Art found out and stopped it, where is the kid? And why is he lying about everything? He would have been a hero. It only makes sense if they both planned to kill the kid. Since he grew up under the same conditions as his sister, is he as screwed up as Angela? If they were both in on it, what were they fighting about that got her killed? And what about Stonehead? Was she part of it, too? Three psychos who liked to kill kids? What are the odds of that happening?"

Mary Ann shook her head in disgust. "We keep going around in a circle. Everything's a dead end."

Ron's phone rang to break up the conversation. It was forensics, with a preliminary report on the prints found in the van.

"Hey, tell me some good news," Ron pleaded.

"Thought you'd want the information as soon as possible, so here's what we've got so far," said Billy, the forensic tech. "Two unique sets of kids' prints were inside the van. Some adults too, but we haven't had time to match them yet. That's all I have right now. We're going to send the prints through the National Crime Information Center database to see if we get any hits. Check our local database, too."

"Thank you. This helps a lot. Call me when you get the search done."

He hung up the phone and whistled.

"What?" said Mary Ann.

Forensics thinks they found two sets of kids' prints in the van."

"No shit. That puts a whole different light on it. Maybe this thing with the kid has been going on for a while."

Her comment tickled a memory in Ron's brain. Grabbing the murder book, he flipped pages until he found the notes he wanted. "Oh, man," he groaned.

"What?" she said.

Remember when we interviewed the neighbor, and she said she saw Angela with a boy on December seventh?"

"Yeah, so?"

"She also said she saw her earlier in the year with a little girl. I forgot about that." He pounded his head with the side of his fist. "A critical clue was sitting right in front of me."

"Hey, don't beat yourself up. I missed it, too."

He took a deep breath and blew it out. "So let's say this has been going on for a while. Angela gets these two kids from somewhere, then hands them off to Art or they both take the kids somewhere, perhaps to Stonehead. So either we have a couple of serial killers here, or they did something else with the kids. It makes kidnapping for ransom unlikely as a motive. There are very few cases of multiple child kidnappings for ransom. Almost all of them get caught after the first one. Since she didn't like kids, I kinda doubt she was babysitting."

Mary Ann thought of an explanation and slapped her hand down on her desk. "Suppose they weren't killing the kids, but selling them?"

Ron drummed his fingers on the arm of his chair. "It sort of fits," he admitted. "Her job gives her access to kids. Her brother's the bag man who sells them off. Doesn't explain Stonehead's involvement, though."

"She's a lawyer. Perhaps she took care of the paperwork, made it look like the kids were being legally adopted."

"Where were the kids coming from? We checked missing persons and nobody reported any missing. The obvious answer is through Child Services, but they said every kid is tracked from the moment they get them."

"Didn't she assign the kids to the caseworkers? Suppose she picked a kid nobody cared about, erased all the records in the database, and took him home."

"If she did, she took tremendous risks," he replied. "I can think of a zillion things that could go wrong with a scheme like that. Plus, from what her supervisor said, she didn't seem the type to take risks of that order."

"Maybe she was so screwed up in the head it kind of overrode her common sense," Mary Ann offered.

"We've got to find out if she could keep these kids out of the database. I would think Child Services would have safeguards to make sure that couldn't happen. And if they were selling the kids, who did they sell them to?"

Mary Ann had no answer to that question. Ron

called forensics and asked them to return to Angela's house to check for fingerprints in the bedroom with the deadbolt on the door. That room of the house suffered less damage, so prints might still be there. If they could match the prints in the van to prints in the house, it would prove Art and Angela both had the kid at some point and be pretty damning evidence they worked together.

Towards three o'clock, Mary Ann received an email from the phone company with Stonehead's phone records. A phone call at six ten p.m. on December seventh to a Dorothy Stonehead lasted until seven twenty-five. There were no calls to the burner phone, or to Art's cell phone.

"That just about rules Stonehead out as the killer," Ron declared, "and still no proof she even knows Art. So how does she fit in?"

Chapter Thirty-Two

January 23rd

A forensics team went back out to Angela's house the following morning, checking for prints in the bedroom. As instructed, they paid special attention to areas like doorknobs and light switches, things that kids would likely touch. Back at the office, Ron was trying to track down other neighbors on Angela's street. Not an easy task, given the recent evacuation. Christ knew where they might have gone. His phone chirped with a call from Billy.

"Good news! We found a few good prints on the bedroom wall by the light switch."

"Excellent," Ron said. "When can you tell me if they match the ones in the van?"

"Take a couple of days; things are pretty backed up at the lab."

"I don't have a couple of days. Kids are missing, and I need a match so I can go after Garcia. Need I remind you this is a murder investigation?"

Billy hedged his answer. "I'll call in some favors, but the best I can do is day after tomorrow."

"Do what you can. Call me as soon as you have something."

Ron slumped in his chair, rolling a pencil between his thumb and forefinger. Finally, some hard evidence might exist to tie Garcia to the missing kid. He needed something, anything. They were eighteen days into the investigation and knew little more than they did on day one. Every day that went by made it less likely they would solve the case. It had morphed way beyond anything expected, and the pressure for results was mounting.

If the prints didn't match those in the van, the case was going nowhere.

Chapter Thirty-Three

March 2017

It was a rainy Saturday at the Stagger Inn. Inside the bar, patrons drank beer and ate wings, entertained by the March Madness basketball playoffs on the big screen TVs. Cheers and groans filled the room every time one team scored a point. Because of the rain, many fans stayed home, watching the games from the comfort of an easy chair and frig filled with brews. There were plenty of empty tables to choose from.

Art got there early and picked out a booth in the back, away from the crowd. He sat with his back to the wall and waited for his contact to appear. The smell of burgers cooking on the grill made his stomach growl.

While desperately trying to please his sister by finding someone who would be interested in older kids, he saw a TV documentary on the dark web, a part of the Internet invisible to anyone without the proper software. It was full of secret websites and blogs which required passwords to access. An amazing world, hidden in plain sight. Most of the content lived on servers in sketchy areas all over the world, outside the jurisdiction of American law enforcement. This looked like the answer to his prayers.

Art bought the necessary equipment and software, then spent the first week just browsing around to identify the sites interested in children. He followed link after link, trying to drill down, find the right people. Eventually, he found Teddy Bear Fantasies.

Teddy Bear advertised all sorts of sexual depravity and was very interested in his proposition. Negotiations started but didn't get far. As often happens when two people unknown to each other are doing illegal things, there was a question of trust. The government targeted perceived child traffickers relentlessly with sting operations. The price could be twenty years in prison if caught. No one wanted to say anything incriminating on the Internet. To break the impasse, Art arranged a face-to-face meeting at his old watering hole.

The front door swung open, and a man entered, carrying a black briefcase in his left hand. He fit the description provided: black trench coat over a flannel shirt and a pair of blue jeans. Despite the rain, he had no hat, and his scalp glistened with water.

He was short, but muscular, with a thick neck and hair shaved close to his scalp, like a military cut. His eyes, sunken in his skull, missed nothing. A hawk nose gave him a menacing look.

Scanning the room, his gaze found Art. "You Frank?" he asked. This was the alias Art gave him.

"Yeah, you Bob?"

"Yeah."

Both men shook hands. Bob slid into the booth opposite him. The server hustled over to take his order, a diet coke. The two men sat studying each other until she reappeared with his drink.

He raised his glass. "Here's to a long and profitable partnership."

After sipping their drinks for a few moments, it was

time to get down to business.

Bob spoke first. "Okay, you say you can deliver the goods I'm interested in. I want you to tell me how you're getting the goods."

Art shook his head. "I can't tell you that. Got to protect my source. Let's just say I check the goods out, make sure nobody will miss 'em. No records. They don't exist."

He had more questions. "This sounds too good to be true. What about the parents and relatives? What makes you think nobody will be looking for them?"

"Like I said, I check out their history. Got ways to do that. Anyone not meetin' the criteria gets a pass."

Bob took a long drink of his diet coke, mulling it over. "This smells like a setup."

Art shrugged. "How do I know you ain't the FBI?"

His new friend sat back and smiled. "I'm not a cop. We have clients all over the world. Rich people with a certain lifestyle they like to maintain and can afford. Wish I had some references, but these people demand secrecy. I'm just the middleman, delivering the goods, getting paid, and then I never see them again. You've seen my company on the web, so you understand what happens."

"Yeah, a bunch of sick fucks. You ever find people who want to adopt for real?"

Bob shook his head. "I'll need a picture of the goods before I can commit to buy. If there's no interest from my clients, then there's no deal."

This wouldn't work. The picture presented no problem. Angie would take it and send it to him. The problem was what to do with the kid if Bob took a pass on the action. The kid would need to be put back into the system, quickly. They couldn't hold on to a kid nobody wanted. Time was of the essence. Bob would have to make his decision immediately.

"Okay, I can send you a pic, but you got only ninety minutes to decide. After that, the goods go elsewhere. I get paid in full at delivery; cash only, nothing over C-notes."

"Of course, cash on delivery is standard practice. I can describe the most desirable goods and if you can match that we should have no problems."

They talked for another hour, ironing out details of how they would do the exchange. When they finished, Bob removed a pair of gloves from his trench coat and put them on, taking pen and paper from inside his briefcase. He wrote a list of things on the paper, folded it, and handed it to him.

"Here's a list of what I want now. It may change from time to time. I'll contact you if that happens. There's my number. Call me anytime, day or night."

"I'll be in touch," he replied

Nodding, he rose and left the bar, taking the glass he had been drinking from with him. *Paranoid little prick*, Art thought. But it was not something a cop would do.

As agreed, he waited another five minutes to give his new partner time to leave the parking lot. Outside, rain fell as he ran to his car. He called Angela. "Hey, good news. "I found a guy who can take those packages we talked 'bout."

"Really?" She sounded skeptical .

"Yeah, I jus' had a meetin' with him and he's interested. I'm comin' over to give you the details."

****

After Bob Hackman reached his car, he retrieved a

pair of binoculars from the front seat, and melted into the shadows at the edge of the parking lot. He watched Art leave the bar and run through the rain. As he pulled out of the lot, Bob raised the binoculars and copied down his license plate.

He was nervous about where the kids were coming from. For various reasons, there were always kids with no parents or relatives to claim them. This could be the source, but they usually were cared for by the state until they were adopted or aged out at eighteen. It would require help from someone pretty high in the government to make one of those kids disappear.

Alternatively, the kids could be coming from teenage mothers who did not want a kid at that point in their lives. These kids were in high demand, and legitimate companies specialized in finding them. Everything would have to be done legally, so they would never do business with Frank. It was necessary to learn more about his new friend before things went any further. His employer would demand it.

The following Monday, he called his contact at the DMV, gave him the plate number, and got the information he sought. Frank was really Art Garcia, and he lived in Santa Maria. The fake name did not alarm Bob. Some guys needed to protect themselves when meeting a stranger under dangerous circumstances.

Now that he had an actual name, he dug deeper, discovering Garcia owned a business, AG Consulting. It appeared to be making money; based upon some tax returns he reviewed by hacking into the state's computer system. He found no information about the business itself—it was unadvertised in any manner. Not something a legitimate consultant would do, so it was a front for something else.

He roamed the streets, talking to the druggies and prostitutes. "Do you know a guy named Art?" he would ask, and sometimes they did.

"Why you lookin' for him?" replied a ragged crack head.

"Heard he can hook you up. Get you anything you want," Bob stated.

"I might have heard of the guy, but my memory ain't what it used to be."

Bob passed him a twenty. "Does this help you remember?"

The crack head snatched the bill out of his hand and gave a toothless grin. "In Santa Barbara there's a dealer calls himself Art. That's all I know. You ask around downtown, somebody tell you where to find him."

Bob reached into his pocket and removed a picture taken secretly during the meeting at the bar. "Is this the guy?"

"Yeah, that's him."

This fleshed out the background. Art made his living as a drug dealer who used his consulting business to launder money. The adoption scam might be a new idea to make more money, or maybe he was recruited into it by someone else. The unanswered question remained. Where were the kids coming from? One possibility—he sold to drug addicts. They had children, and sometimes sold them for the drugs they craved.

Bob staked out his friend's house for a few days to see if anyone else lived there. He kept his distance to avoid being spotted, but with a pair of high-powered binoculars he had no trouble observing. Other than a dog, there appeared to be no other tenants.

The house's excellent location, well protected at the top of a small, rounded hill providing splendid views in any direction, impressed him. Cameras hung on the eves of each side of the house. Security bars covered all the windows and doors. The dog roamed the yard unleashed but did not venture far from the house.

It would be very difficult to penetrate without being seen. If you got to the house undetected by the cameras, the bars on the windows would have to be dealt with, as well as the dog. And once inside, who knew what other defenses might be encountered? This was a safe house, designed for someone who needed protection. More confirmation that a career drug dealer lived there.

Satisfied his potential partner was not working with law enforcement, he wrote up his report and sent it off to his superiors via encrypted email. He would await their instructions before he did any business with Art Garcia.

Chapter Thirty-Four

Angela was waiting for her brother by the garage door with a cold beer in her hand. After a few swallows, he followed her into the family room, flopped down in an easy chair and filled her in on his conversation with Bob. "So that's it. This ain't like adoption. These kids get sold to the highest bidder, flown out of the country, and become somebody's slave. The kid's life is over. I feel kinda bad about it, but the pay is good. You okay with that?"

She appeared lost in thought, chewing on her bottom lip.

"Angie?" he asked after she didn't respond.

Her head came back; she let out a deep sigh. "Look, I don't give a shit what happens to the kids, but I don't like giving this guy the power to veto the delivery. I'm taking a huge chance just getting the kid, and if he turns us down, I have to put the kid back into the system like nothing happened. What if word got out the kid was at my house? That would get me fired."

"Relax, it's cool. I only gave him ninety minutes to decide. Jus' take the kid for ice cream or somethin' 'til we hear. Nothin' suspicious 'bout that."

"What do you know about him? Can we trust him not to set us up?"

Art explained about the dark web, and how he had used it to find Bob.

She exploded. "So all you have on this guy is what you saw on the web?"

His face flushed red, stung because once again he had failed to please her. All he wanted was a little praise, some recognition. Show him a little respect, for once. He'd been the one doing all the legwork, pretending to be one of those sick perverts, just to find the right guy to work with. She'd been sitting on her ass the whole time, doing nothing.

"Angie," he snapped. "I can't go 'round askin' for references. The guy's a criminal, for Christ's sake. I talked to him for hours, and my gut tells me he's legit. I'm the one takin' the risk when I do the exchange. He don't know about you."

"Oh, really?" she retorted. "If you get busted, how long you think it will be before they figure out where you got the kid?"

He had no answer for that.

"So you want to call it off?" he asked.

Pacing back and forth across the living room, she tried to decide. She doubted this guy was trustworthy. But if they were being setup, it was a very sophisticated trap. If she said no to this, her brother would most likely give up searching and her dream of early retirement would be over. The rest of her life would be spent working with those horrible kids and their screwed-up parents. Even thinking about that made her feel sick to her stomach. But what alternative did she have? Quitting her job was not the answer. That would cut off her source of kids, and her entire income would go away. She would be starting over from the bottom, in some other crappy job she wouldn't like, and that didn't appeal to her either.

Then she thought of a plan. "Okay, Art, I'm going

to trust you on this. If you screw this up, we're both going down. Be in jail for the rest of our lives." She gave him a stern look. "But I want to test this guy first. Here's what we're going to do."

She explained the test. It impressed him. If Bob took the bait, they would kill the whole deal before the exchange, and never see him again.

Art waited almost a month before he contacted Bob. He did not want him to think it was easy to find a kid at a moment's notice. As they had agreed, he sent an encrypted email, along with a picture and a brief history of an eight-year-old girl named Danielle. The price was set at thirty thousand. He reminded Bob he had ninety minutes to decide. After he hit the send button, there was nothing to do but wait.

Angela provided Danielle's picture from an old case file. The picture was quite unflattering. In it, the girl's uncombed hair stuck out in all directions. Large ears protruded from the sides of her head like rudders. Freckles dotted her pale white skin. Her nose, in contrast to her ears, appeared too small for her face. She was grinning at the camera, showing a row of yellow crooked teeth. A dirty shirt, too large for her, hung like a bag on her thin frame over a pair of ripped, threadbare jeans. She wore flip-flops for shoes.

The theory was if Bob wanted kids to sell to rich perverts, he would be uninterested in an ugly one. So if he said yes to Danielle, the odds were good it was a setup. If this happened, they would cut ties with him. Art had never given him any personal information other than his phone number. So all he had to do was dispose of his burner phone and walk away. At that point, they had done nothing illegal.

Following this somewhat twisted logic, if he declined to take the kid, he would pass their test and be considered trustworthy. It wasn't a foolproof test, but better than blindly accepting his story.

When the allotted ninety-minute deadline passed with no response, the siblings celebrated with a six-pack of beer. Angela started looking for real candidates.

It took her only a few weeks to find one. Art followed the same protocol and sent another email. This time, it was a five-year-old Hispanic girl named Francesca, who looked cute and cleaned up much better than Danielle. They set a price of forty thousand. Almost ninety minutes elapsed before they received a reply. It was just one word: "Accepted".

The following morning, he drove his van into Angela's garage, closing the garage door behind him. His sister met him there, looking nervous, unable to stand still, bags under her eyes from lack of sleep.

He grinned, trying to give her the impression he had everything under control. In reality, he had slept little the previous night, either, thinking of all the things that could go wrong.

"Got it all fixed. We hook up at ten. He gives me the money, I give him the kid. End of story."

For once, he was the center of attention, and enjoying it. Finally, a chance to earn his sister's respect.

Angela searched her brother's face. "I've been up all night with the whinny brat trying to get her to sleep. She wanted her mother. What could I do? Her mother is dead. She might cry when she's with you, wanting to go home or something. Are you sure about this? Is your gut still telling you this is all legit? I'm freaked out right now."

He gave his sister's shoulder a squeeze. "I'm sure.

Gonna have my pistol, just in case, but I think he wants to do this deal as bad as we do. Soon as it's done, we'll hook up. If I don't say the code word first thing, or you don't hear from me by noon, get out of town quick as you can. If I get busted, you might not have a lot of time before they find out 'bout you, so don't wait 'round. Go somewhere safe."

With a nod, she led her brother down the hall to the spare bedroom, and introduced Francesca to Frank, the name Art wanted to use. "He's going to take you for a ride," she explained.

The child inspected him suspiciously. "Is he going to take me home?"

Angela glanced at her brother. "Sure honey, he's going to do that. You just have to be a good girl while he's driving, okay?"

Francesca studied him but gave no sign she was ready to leave. He squatted down to her level. "Hey, you like chocolate? I got a candy bar in the van."

She brightened. "Okay."

He straightened and held out his hand. They took kid steps out to the garage together. Sliding the side door of the van open, he helped Francesca climb in. After buckling her seat belt, he rummaged around in the center console, producing the chocolate bar. She clapped her hands, grabbed it, and began peeling off the wrapper. He slid the door shut and faced his sister.

"This is it. Stay by the phone. Should be a done deal by ten thirty."

He gave her a wink, climbed into the van, and backed out of the garage.

Chapter Thirty-Five

Summer 2017

During the long summer, Angela kidnapped one more baby and two older kids. The older kids were both girls, seven and twelve. The exchange with the seven-year-old went well. Twelve-year-old Natalie was a different matter. She was streetwise beyond her years, having been bounced around from place to place since the age of four, seeing and hearing a lot of bad things. Raped by her father on her seventh birthday, she had no respect for authority, but plenty of hatred for all adults.

Angela should have sent this troublemaker on into the judicial system, but all the previous exchanges had gone well, so she was overconfident. Natalie was lured into the house with the explanation she would just be there for the night, but it went downhill from there. She didn't like being locked in a bedroom with bars on the window. When Angela brought her dinner, she threw it back at her, calling her every foul name in the book. She spent the following hours kicking the door in a vain attempt to break out.

The next morning, when Art arrived for the pickup, she sensed something wrong and refused to leave the bedroom. An all-out brawl ensued. She threw a lamp, which he dodged, and it shattered on the wall behind him. Before she could find anything else to throw, he tackled her onto the bed, pinning her down, while Angela wrapped duct tape around her arms and legs.

Together, the siblings carried Natalie out to the garage. The girl, perhaps thinking someone might hear her there, began screaming.

"Okay, that's it," Art said.

He tore off a piece of duct tape and placed it over the twelve-year-old's mouth. "All you doin' is makin' this harder on yourself," he said sternly. "Nobody gonna hurt you."

The two of them lifted her onto the floor of the van and slammed shut the door. Both siblings, panting from the struggle, stopped to rest.

"I've got to be more selective with these older kids," Angela said. "They know too much."

Chapter Thirty-Six

January 24th

Ron sat at his desk, idly tapping out a tune in his head with a pencil. Time was at a standstill. He thought of nothing else but the safe. His only chance to solve the case might be in there. Or it might be a red herring containing nothing of significance. There was another two hours to go before the locksmith came to open it. The wait was killing him.

A soft ping from his computer announced the arrival of an email. It was the ballistics report on Garcia's pistol. A bullet had been fired from it into a tank of water. Then the distinctive markings on it had been compared to the markings on the bullet that killed Angela. The results indicated Garcia's pistol was not the gun used during the murder.

Of course. It would have been too easy if the bullets had matched. This case was going to drag on and on and maybe never be solved.

He shared the report with Mary Ann, who made a sour face, but had no comment.

About nine o'clock, Billy from forensics called. "Okay," he said, sounding exhausted. "You owe me big time. I called in all kinds of favors to get those prints run. Just got the report, and guess what?"

"Speak to me," said Ron.

"A print matched one we got from the van."

"That is good news, Billy. Any idea who it is?"

"Nothing yet. The prints are being run through the databases now. If I hear something this afternoon, I'll let you know."

"What?" said Mary Ann when the call ended.

"We got a match on a print in the house with one in the van."

"Yes!" she said. "Now if we can just get a name…"

"They're still working on it, but we've got solid proof now that Art and Angela worked together."

"Doing what?"

He shrugged. "Let's hope we'll find evidence of that in the safe."

"Oh," she said, remembering something. "Alvarez left a message last night that he sent copies of the will to Garcia and Stonehead. Felt he couldn't wait any longer. Some fiduciary duty crap. Art must have it by now, so he knows he didn't inherit the property."

Ron frowned. "If I was Stonehead, I'd be staying away from dark places."

The detectives busied themselves preparing for the locksmith. The safe was stored in a cramped evidence room, so a forklift was requisitioned to move it to the loading dock in the back of the building, where there was more space. A camera was set up on a tripod, ready to record everything.

Larry, the locksmith, appeared promptly at ten and checked out the safe. "This is a Steel Fortress Model 500, with four two-inch bolts locking the door onto the frame. The easiest way to open this is to drill the keypad out. That's hardened steel around it, so it's going to take a while. You guys might want to go relax somewhere while I work on it."

Disgruntled there would be no immediate discoveries, the detectives returned to their desks.

Two hours later, Larry appeared and announced it was time to open the safe. They all marched back out to the loading dock.

The safe's keypad lay on the ground, exposing a pair of wires inside the door of the safe. He had spliced another pair of wires on to them. They ran along the floor to a small battery pack sitting on a table. The acrid smell of burned metal permeated the air.

Ron started recording, and with everyone gathered around, Larry flipped a switch on the battery pack. An audible clicking sound indicated the safe unlocked. Stepping forward, he grasped the wheel mounted on the door, and spun it counterclockwise. The two-inch bolts drew back into the door. With a flourish, the locksmith swung it open. The detectives leaned forward, trying to see what was inside.

Two shelves occupied the top of the safe. Below them were two large drawers. Attention immediately focused on the top shelf where piles of currency held together with rubber bands rested.

Mary Ann whistled. "Lot of money there."

"Let's see what else is in here," replied Ron. "Then we can count it."

The second shelf was empty. He pulled out the drawer beneath it. Inside, four large manila envelopes took up all the space. He removed each one and laid them on a table next to the safe. The first envelope contained the deed to Angela's house, recorded when her father died and willed her the house. Mary Ann took a picture of it and scribbled down a note on a pad of paper. The second envelope contained Angela's will. The third, a life insurance policy in the amount of $10,000 issued through the county. Art Garcia was named as the beneficiary. The last envelope contained a homeowner's insurance policy.

When it was all documented, Ron slid the top drawer back into the safe and pulled out the bottom drawer. It contained only one item, a small black notebook. Picking it up, he fanned the pages. It appeared to be blank except for the first page, which contained seven lines of figures. The first line read "160223PS30", the second "160414PS25", and so on. The seventh and final line said "170729AG20". No explanation of what it meant.

He passed the notebook to Mary Ann. "Any idea what this means?"

She studied the numbers, then took out her phone and took a picture. "Obviously some kind of code. After we're done here, maybe we can figure it out."

Ron returned to the safe. There was nothing else in it. He slipped all the documents into evidence bags. The bundles of cash, removed one at a time from the safe, got stuffed into several larger evidence bags. "Let's take this money inside where we can count it in a more secure location."

They settled down in one of the interrogation rooms, where they could record the counting of the money. Ron took one bundle of cash at a time from the bag, slipped off the rubber band, and counted it on the table. When he finished, Mary Ann made a note of the amount on her pad. After slipping the rubber band back on the cash, the next bundle was retrieved from the bag and the counting process started again. Very slow going, but after an hour and a half the bags were empty. Mary Ann totaled up her figures. The safe contained $165,000. There was nothing more to inventory. After logging in the contents of the safe as evidence, the detectives returned to their desks.

Chapter Thirty-Seven

"This is way too much money for Angela to have saved from her salary," Ron pointed out.

"I agree," Mary Ann said, leaning back in her chair. "Child Services doesn't pay much, and she still had a mortgage and all her other bills to pay. If this money was saved legitimately, wouldn't she put it in the bank where it would earn interest?"

Ron nodded. "She might've worried about creating a paper trail to trace the money. I'm thinking the money came from trafficking, but that's a lot of money for just two kids."

"This little black notebook might be a log of some sort," she declared. "There are seven entries. Let's see if we can figure out the code."

They hunched over their desks, scrutinizing the figures. After a few minutes, Mary Ann said, "The first six numbers look like dates written European style. The first two digits might be the year since they only go from 16 to 17. If that's right, then the next two digits are the month, and the next two are the day."

"Yeah, that fits. The next two letters are PS or AG. Where have we seen this before?" He answered his own question. "Why, it's the initials of our two suspects, Patsy Stonehead and Art Garcia."

She gave him a high five. "This is a piece of information that ties them both to Angela. But what do the last two figures represent?"

"There are only three different numbers: ten, twenty-five, and thirty. So it varied little from one entry to another." He had an idea. "How much is this if we add all the numbers?"

Mary Ann dragged out her calculator and started punching keys. "It totals up to one hundred seventy."

"We recovered one hundred sixty-five thousand from the safe, so I'll bet this is the amount she got for each kid, leaving off the three zeros at the end," he said. "She might have spent part of it, which is why it doesn't match. There's no entry for January seventh though, when the neighbor saw her with a kid."

"That all makes sense to me," said Mary Ann. "Maybe she never had time to add the eighth entry into her book before she died. If we are correct, we're not looking for two missing kids, we're looking for eight." When her partner made no response, Mary Ann glanced at him. He appeared to be far away, thinking of something else. "Ron?"

"What if they got Becky?" he mumbled, staring straight ahead.

"What? Oh no, that's not possible. That happened a long time ago."

"I'll make them tell me what happened. Maybe she's still alive."

Alarmed, she said, "Ron, look at me!"

He turned slowly, looking at her with vacant eyes.

"Garcia and Stonehead couldn't have done it. They were children when Becky went missing."

When he still said nothing, she repeated the facts. "Ron, it's not your sister."

Chapter Thirty-Eight

October 1994

1994, a memorable year for Ron, who turned sixteen and finally got the driver's license he coveted. No more begging rides from his older friends and parents. He bought a beat up Ford that got him to school and back, and settled into high school life. He excelled in sports and became popular with the girls, prerequisites to becoming a big man on campus.

His sister, three years younger and a royal pest, was in junior high. He avoided her as much as possible. However, as part of the bargain with his parents to allow him to get a car, he agreed to pick her up on his way home from school every day. He didn't always do this, as he often had important things to do after school that didn't involve her. This would lead to many arguments between them. Becky would be in a huff because she had to *walk* home, which was humiliating, since all of her friends had rides.

Their parents mediated, and Ron would promise it would not happen again, but it always did, eventually. He had a social life, which somebody in junior high could never understand. It took her only twenty minutes to walk home, so what was the big deal?

He found out what the big deal was that fall. One day after school, on his way to the parking lot, he bumped into a girl he wanted to date. Trying to make an impression on her, he stopped to chat. An hour later, he checked his watch and realized he blew it again.

Cruising by the junior high, he had little hope his sister would still be there. The school was deserted. Resigned to another argument, he glumly motored on home to face the music.

He entered the house through the garage, hoping to sneak upstairs to his room and avoid his sister. Instead, he found his mother, busy preparing dinner in the kitchen. Turning to him, she wiped her hands on her apron, searching for something behind him. "Where's Becky?"

"Aw, Mom, I got tied up after school and lost track of the time. I cruised by her school but didn't see her. She must have walked home. Did you check her room?"

That began the worst day of his life. A quick search of the house and yard yielded no sign of Becky. The increasingly frantic calls to her friends elicited only one bit of information: she was last seen waiting for her brother in front of the school.

Ron drove around aimlessly, checking every street between her school and home. *This can't be happening.* She's just mad, hiding to make me freak out. But by nightfall, he had to admit that something far more serious was happening.

The police responded, and a proper search began. Family friends put up flyers on all the streetlights, and her picture appeared on the local news. A large reward for information elicited no leads. Days, then weeks, and finally months flew by. Becky disappeared from their lives forever.

He carried the guilt for a long time, unmotivated to

do anything. He quit sports, withdrew from his friends, and struggled to focus in class. Everyone in school knew what happened, and he became an object of pity. *Why is he so weird?* a kid new to school would ask.

Oh, he's the guy whose sister disappeared when he forgot to pick her up after school.

His parents were careful never to blame him for what happened. Becky was being stalked, they said. The stalker had already decided to take her, just waiting for an opportunity, and if it hadn't been then, it would have been some other time when she was alone.

Ron wondered how they knew this. Maybe the pervert drove around aimlessly, looking for targets, and saw her walking home. Grabbed her right off the street. Wouldn't have happened at all if he'd picked her up like he promised.

He watched his mother withdraw into her shell. Rarely speaking, she spent more and more time alone in her room or on long walks. Her overwhelming sadness only fed the guilt that Ron carried every day.

His father finally broke through his despair. "You can make something good out of this," he said.

"Dad, I fucked up. How can anything good come from that?"

"You've always wanted to be a cop, right?"

He nodded grudgingly.

"Use this as motivation to become the best cop in the world. Protect other kids from this happening to them. Keep people safe and put bad people in jail where they can't hurt anyone ever again. You can make a difference."

Chapter Thirty-Nine

January 24th

You can make a difference.

Ron took those words to heart, joined the police force, and busted his ass to make detective. When he finally made it, he hungered for cases that involved protecting innocent kids from the nightmare his sister endured. Strangely enough, in the years since he joined the force, not one case involving a child kidnapping happened on his watch. He buried the guilt and concentrated on police work.

And now eight kids had gone missing with no clue what happened to them. It was Becky all over again. The guilt flooded back.

He heard a voice through the fog in his brain.

"They didn't do it," Mary Ann repeated, in his face now and touching his arm, trying to get his attention. "Do you understand?"

Slowly, he focused his gaze on her. "Somebody knows what happened."

"It was almost thirty years ago," Mary Ann stressed. "This is a totally different case, Ron. We've got solid information to work with. If this is a log of the kids, we have dates of when seven kidnappings occurred. Let's go back and check the records at Child Services to see if we can get some names. We'll get a search warrant for

Stonehead's house, too."

Ron was silent for a moment. Then he took a deep breath and snapped back to reality. "I'm sorry. I lost it there for a minute. Eight kids are gone, just like Becky. I'm supposed to be protecting them, and I've done nothing."

Mary Ann sighed. "We have to stay focused. We're getting new information that can help us break this case."

He couldn't let it go. Not completely. "I don't understand how eight kids can go missing and no one says one word about it. Are there more people involved and they're covering it up somehow? If we're right about this, it might get pretty heavy and end some careers. We need to update the lieutenant."

The musty smell from Warner's office seeped out into the hall. He sat, half buried, behind a pile of folders. His head snapped up when the detectives knocked on his door. They walked in and took the two chairs on the other side of his desk. "Tell me you solved the Garcia case."

Ron explained the notebook evidence found in the safe; how the initials AG and PS might implicate Art Garcia and Patsy Stonehead, and how it looked like as many as eight kids might have disappeared over the last two years.

"Eight?" Warner exclaimed. "How is that possible? Somebody had to be watching them."

Ron saw an opportunity to speak his mind. "That's the problem, LT. We need to ask questions to the people who run Child Services and their police contacts. Depending on what we find, the investigation might spread to other departments, and that means the politicians will run for cover. There might be a lot of pushbacks to bury this. Nobody will want to talk. And if the media finds out what's going on, they're going to crucify us."

Warner massaged his temples. His lips clamped in a thin line; his eyes were filled with worry. "We've got no choice here," he declared. "Those eight kids deserve justice. They're still out there somewhere. I'm going to call the Chief and ask him to set up a meeting with Director Duncan over in Child Services. We need to keep a lid on this as long as possible, so I'm telling both of you not to discuss this with anybody at all. I don't want you talking to anyone in Child Services yet. Am I clear?"

Ron and Mary Ann nodded.

"Okay. Now get out of here and let me make the call. Shut the door on your way out."

Back at their desks, Mary Ann looked worried. "We're screwed, aren't we?"

"Yeah, everybody's going to treat us like pariahs," Ron muttered. "Whomever didn't do their job right and allowed those eight kids to disappear needs to go to jail. Anybody with any ties to this cluster fuck will try to spin things to deflect the blame off themselves and onto someone else."

Mary Ann raised her hand like she wanted to say something. He ignored it. "I've seen this happen before. Do not cooperate if you're asked to do or say something you're not comfortable with. If we play that game, we'll go down with the rest of them. We've got to stick to the facts, Mary Ann, and let others worry about the fallout." He gazed intently at her. "I need to know something partner. Do you have my back?"

Ron was asking her if she would risk her career to clear the case. He knew she was ambitious, hoping someday to be chief, and she might lose that opportunity by rocking the boat. She had enemies in the department, and they watched her, waiting for a slipup. On the other hand, what kind of leader would she be if she ducked for cover at the first sign of trouble?

She didn't hesitate. "This may kill my career here, but I don't give a damn. I keep thinking what if it had been Tomas? Nobody else is going to care about those kids except us. So yeah, I've got your back. If we go down, we do it together."

Chapter Forty

A call from Billy interrupted the conversation. "We ran those kids prints through everything we had, and got a hit, out of our own local database. They belong to a Natalie Martinez, twelve years old, in and out of juvie hall since she was four. Parents are deceased, no known relatives. She ran away from foster care on May nineteenth. During a police sweep of an abandoned building on May twentieth, they discovered her hiding in a closet. She was transferred to Child Services the same day. After that, she became their responsibility."

Ron closed his eyes, rubbing a fingertip over his brow. "Who in Child Services took the kid?"

"No idea. Sergeant Crone handles all the turnovers. You need to talk to him. He should have that information."

"Thanks, Billy, I owe you one."

"Hah! You owe me two."

After hanging up, Ron relayed the new information to Mary Ann, who then pulled a copy of Angela's list out of her desk drawer. "We got an entry that coincides with the dates from Billy: 170521AG10".

"Bingo," he said. "Looks like Garcia picked up Natalie on May twenty-first." He hesitated. "You know, the LT said nothing about talking to cops."

She smiled. By chance, Sergeant Crone worked in the same building.

They kicked around ideas, settling on Mary Ann pretending to be gathering information for a paper she was writing for a class. Ron would stay behind.

"Say nothing about the case," he said. "Make it sound routine so he won't get suspicious."

****

Mary Ann picked up a notebook and proceeded to the lunchroom to refresh her coffee. On the way back, she detoured to the other end of the building where Sergeant Tony Crone worked. He was hunched over his keyboard, oblivious to the surrounding noise, as she approached.

"Hey Tony, you got a minute?"

He glanced up, surprise on his face. "Mary Ann! What brings you to the dark side? You tired of looking at that ugly partner of yours?"

She laughed. "I'm used to him now, even though he is ugly. Sorry to interrupt, I'm taking this class on the Juvenile Justice System. I'm writing a paper on what happens to abandoned kids. I've been told you are the guy to talk to about that."

Tony grunted and slouched in his chair. "I'm only involved in a small piece of it. When the patrols find a kid with no parents or relatives, they turn the kid over to me. I contact Child Services to come pick up the kid. End of story."

"So what happens then?"

"The kid becomes the responsibility of Child Services, who then tries to find any relatives. If that's unsuccessful, the kid gets processed into the system for a court hearing. I know very little about how it works. I'd talk to them if I was you."

"Yeah, it's my next stop. So, do you call the same

person at Child Services every time, or is it whoever answers the phone?"

"The process is I call my contact over there, who makes plans to pick up the kid. Sometimes it would be her and sometimes another person."

"Okay," Mary Ann said evenly. "Guess I should go talk to her next. What's the name?"

He hesitated. "Well, you can't talk to her because she's dead. Her name was Angela Garcia." He looked at her quizzically. "Hey, didn't you and Ron catch that case?"

She pretended ignorance. "Yeah, it's our case all right. She was your contact? Small world. Who are you dealing with now?"

"Child Services hasn't named her replacement yet, so I'm dealing with her supervisor, Ricardo Rodriguez."

She scribbled in her notebook. "I'll hook up with him to get the rest of the story. I've got one last question. How many abandoned kids do you estimate come through the door every year?"

He scratched his head. "It varies, depending on the economy. The worse it gets, the more kids we see. Check our database. You can get a count for whatever period you're looking at."

"Got it. Hey thanks Tony. I owe you one. This paper is due next week and I haven't even started it yet. Need to hustle on this one. See you around." She waved and strolled back toward her desk.

****

Neither Ron nor Mary Ann knew a police database of abandoned kids even existed. They had never had occasion to use it. He searched around on his computer, flipping from screen to screen until he located it. After typing in the name Natalie Martinez in the search box, her file flashed onto the screen. The last notes, written by Crone on May 20th, documented that Angela Garcia from Child Services took custody of Natalie, essentially closing the case at the law enforcement end. He printed out a copy and added it to the murder book. Adding to his overall agitation, the search function only allowed searches by name or case number, not date. Since he didn't have names for the other kids, he was stuck.

"Damn it!" he swore. "We're right there, ready to crack this wide open, and I'm stuck in this damn database."

"Maybe the data geeks have a trick so we could search by date," Mary Ann replied.

"It's possible," said Ron, unconvinced, "but the LT will have to expedite it. We've got no juice with them. All kinds of questions about why we need it are going to be asked and make it impossible to keep this a secret for much longer."

"Now we know where Angela got the kids and why she did it," Mary Ann said. "We still don't understand why they aren't in the Child Services database, what happened to them, and whether they are still alive. Only Art Garcia or Stonehead can provide answers to those questions. But we've got enough to charge him with kidnapping Natalie."

"Yeah, I agree," he said. "There's no logical explanation for why her fingerprints would be in his van. If we squeeze him on a kidnapping charge, maybe he'll cave and tell us what happened to the other kids. But what about the murder? There's no evidence he killed his sister. Their lucrative kidnapping business would be a good argument against him killing her. Unless," Ron mused, "they had a falling out over the business, which would be impossible to prove."

"The case against Stonehead is even weaker," Mary Ann said. "We have only the four entries with what might be her initials in the black book to tie her to Angela. There's nothing else to connect her to anything."

"But if the black book is believable, Stonehead helped kidnap four kids," he replied.

If only they could put it all together.

Chapter Forty-One

January 25th

Ron and Mary Ann stood in a small room at police headquarters, monitoring the video feed from the camera in one of the interrogation rooms. In that room were two people—Art Garcia and his lawyer Jim Burnside. The plan was to confront Garcia with the evidence in the safe in a last-ditch effort to extract information or a confession. Ron lured him into appearing by mentioning the safe had been opened and several things of interest found, including a large amount of cash. The mention of cash got Art's attention, but this time he brought his lawyer with him.

The detectives kept them waiting for fifteen minutes, hoping to increase the anxiety level Garcia must be feeling. When they finally entered the room, Burnside introduced himself, and everyone sat down. Art looked around nervously, while his lawyer seemed indifferent, waiting for the interview to begin.

"Thanks for coming in on short notice Mr. Garcia," Ron said. "As I indicated during our phone conversation, we had a locksmith open Angela's safe. We inventoried the contents." He shoved a piece of paper across the table. "Here is a list of what we found. I believe you already have a copy of the will. There was also a copy of the deed to her house when she inherited it from her father, a homeowner's insurance policy, and a $10,000 life insurance policy in which you were named the beneficiary. Finally, the safe contained a considerable amount of cash."

"How much cash?" Garcia asked.

"$165,000."

Burnside spoke. "That money belongs to my client, and he demands you release it to him. It has no relevance to your investigation."

"How do you know it's not relevant to our investigation?" replied Ron.

"Well, it's clearly money Angela Garcia saved over time, and per her will, anything in the safe belongs to my client, Art Garcia."

Ron shook his head. "You are jumping to a conclusion we are not prepared to accept yet. We will not release this money until the end of our investigation. If you want to argue this to the judge, be my guest."

The lawyer slumped back in his chair, looked at his client, and shrugged.

Ron's interrogation continued.

"I have other questions to ask regarding the contents of the safe, starting with Angela's will. The executor of her estate told us he mailed a copy to you, so I'm sure you read it by now. I'm puzzled that Angela named Patsy Stonehead as the primary beneficiary of her estate. I was hoping you might tell us why."

The detectives already knew the answer to this but wanted to goad Garcia into a reaction.

At the mention of Stonehead's name, the man's countenance darkened. "I got no idea. You want to know, ask her yourself."

"Really?" Ron said in a skeptical tone. "Your only

sister never talked about this with you? Doesn't seem right that she just cut you out of the will like that without saying why."

Garcia tensed, but Burnside laid a hand on his shoulder. "My client has answered your question. He knows nothing about this. Let's move on."

"Okay, let's go back to that money in the safe. I checked how much Angela was getting paid by the county and after all her expenses every month there wasn't much left over. Yet somehow she accumulated $165,000. Do you know if she had a second job where she got paid under the table that might account for this? I couldn't find any record of additional income that she paid taxes on."

Mary Ann's phone pinged once, breaking the tension in the room. After quickly glancing at the display, she pushed a button on the phone to send the call to voicemail. "Sorry about that. Forgot to silence my phone."

Everyone's attention returned to Garcia. "She never told me 'bout no second job. Might have been money she got from dad or something."

"So you weren't working with her on anything that might bring in that kind of money?"

"No."

Ron leaned forward, placing his arms on the table. "There was one other item in the safe, a black notebook. In it, there was a list. It's in some kind of code." He held up the notebook for all to see and pushed another piece of paper across the table which contained only the items with the initials "AG". "Here's a copy of the list. Does this refresh your memory?"

Garcia's hands shook slightly as he picked up the

paper. His face went pale as he read it. He put it down quickly. "What's this got to do with me?"

Ron smiled. "It's got everything to do with you. We broke the code. The numbers are dates, European style. Then the letters "AG", which are your initials. That can't be a coincidence. Those numbers after your initials are money, with three zeros left off. That's $60,000 right there. So let's cut the bullshit. Where did the money come from Art?"

As panic filled Garcia's face, Burnside, who had been studying the list, said, "My client has nothing further to say. He disavows any knowledge of the list. I am advising him not to answer any further questions. Unless you plan to arrest him, we are leaving."

Chapter Forty-Two

Art Garcia sat in a private room at his bank, his safe deposit box on a table in front of him. He drove there determined to take action. The interview with Jackson had left him shaken. The box lay open, and he stared at the lotto ticket through its plastic sleeve.

He still seethed with anger over his sister's betrayal in her will. The money in the safe didn't amount to much compared to what he lost on her property. Plus, there was the problem of the entries in the black notebook. This one piece of evidence, which he never dreamed existed, could tie him to the missing kids. The letters "AG" pointed an accusing finger right at him. His sister had screwed him again.

Nothing had gone right for him since the fateful night he got the phone call from Angie on December 7th. All because of the cursed ticket he held in his hands. It was supposed to be his ticket to paradise; but that was a mirage. Might as well throw it away.

He came to the bank in desperation, determined to take the ticket to the lottery officials and claim his prize. But the longer he sat there, the more he realized that opportunity had passed him by. He would be in jail long before the money became available. The detectives had the fingerprints found in his van, the dates in Angela's black book, and the mistake he made with his cell phone. There was also the certainty that given time, they would find out he sold drugs for a living.

Tears trickled down his face. His life was hopeless. One hundred sixty-five thousand dollars in the safe, which everyone except the cops agreed belonged to him—out of reach. The ten thousand on his sister's life insurance amounted to a pittance that wouldn't pay his bills for more than a month or two. The money he had counted on from the sale of Angela's real estate would end up in Stonehead's pocket. Drug sales were crumbling as word on the street spread; he was too hot to do business with. Without an infusion of cash, he would lose his house to foreclosure in a few months. Everything was circling back to where he was a few years ago— broke with no future. A wasted life, that's what it is.

It hadn't started that way. In elementary school, already large for his age, he protected his sister from bullies when she had no friends, receiving only an occasional grudging thanks. At sixteen, she got her first car, a beat-up Chevy with almost 175,000 miles on the odometer. He washed it for her every week, rewarded by getting to sit next to her on "special" occasions when she needed him to carry something. She ignored him for years after she left for college, then suddenly took an interest in his life again, when it suited her purpose.

It all made sense to him now. Angie played him like a fiddle his whole life, telling him what he wanted to hear; and he ate it up, blinded by his need to please her. He realized now what a cold-hearted sociopath she really was. She felt nothing toward him. Used him like a tool, to be thrown away when no longer useful. It hurt down to his soul. After being on his own for so long….he had been betrayed by his sister when she was all he had to hold on to.

With great difficulty, he wrenched himself back to the present. If this ended badly for him, he wasn't going down alone. Patsy Stonehead was somehow involved in this. Did Angela get kids for her, too? Why would she do that when he could sell any kid available? Why hadn't she told him anything about Patsy? And why did she leave the property to her instead of her own brother? Why, why, why? He needed answers, if only for his own peace of mind.

And he knew how to get them.

Chapter Forty-Three

January 26th

Ron and Mary Ann both received calls from the LT at home late Thursday night, telling them to meet in his office by 7:30 a.m. the next day. He would say no more over the phone other than it had something to do with the Garcia case and that the chief was now involved.

Warner was waiting when they arrived, looking tense and worn down. The shit had apparently hit the fan. He ushered both detectives into his office and shut the door after scanning the hallway for eavesdroppers. Waving them to the chairs across from his desk, he sat down heavily, his chair squeaking in protest. He spent a few moments fidgeting, finally making eye contact with the two of them. "Spoke with the chief yesterday. Not a pleasant conversation. Much of it concerned the department looking bad if any of this blows up. It's an election year, and a scandal might…well, you know what could happen."

He paused, studying the detective's faces for a reaction, but got nothing but blank looks.

"After our conversation, he called Duncan over at Child Services, and gave him a summary of what we found so far. Duncan blew a gasket, saying it was impossible eight kids were unaccounted for by his department. He almost accused the chief of lying. Those two have never been friends. After all the mudslinging stopped, they called Farmingham to cover their own asses." Warner stopped talking for a moment to let this sink in.

Liz Farmingham had a reputation as a wily, iron-willed politician, first elected to the Board of Supervisors in 1998. This year she was the Chairperson, a ceremonial job rotated yearly between the supervisors. With a reputation for crushing her enemies without mercy, rumor had it she was laying the groundwork to run for Secretary of State when the incumbent retired next year.

Warner wasn't done. "Farmingham wants to meet with the chief, Duncan, and you two at nine a.m. this morning in her office. Take all your notes and lay the entire case out for her. Hold nothing back or you'll both be looking for new jobs tomorrow. You've got about forty-five minutes to get there. I suggest you haul ass."

Mary Ann cleared her throat. "Are you coming with us, LT?"

He shook his head. "Not invited."

"Who's watching our backs?" Ron asked. "What if they make us the fall guys on this?"

"I don't like it any more than you do. Trust that Chief Newman makes sure it doesn't happen. Now get going."

****

The Board of Supervisors occupied the fourth floor of the County Administration Building on Anapamu Street. It was a rectangular building of modern design, with many windows, and a red tile roof. All five members of the board had offices there, which they decorated to their liking. The meeting was scheduled in a large conference room, used by individual supervisors whenever they wished.

The detectives drove into the parking lot with ten minutes to spare. The lobby was crowded with government employees and the public. They took the elevator to the fourth floor where Newman and Duncan waited in the conference room.

Chief Newman rushed over to shake hands and take them aside in a corner of the room where they had some privacy. He had worked his way up the ranks over a thirty-year career in the police department. Tall and trim in a spotless uniform, his hair had gone white instead of gray. A pair of wire-rimmed glasses perched on a strong nose. Beads of sweat covered his brow as he peered over his glasses at the detectives.

"You guys got everything you need?" he asked in a low voice.

They nodded.

"Okay. Is there anything I should know before we start?"

Ron assumed this meant anything that would make him look bad. "We have found nothing the department did wrong that would cause this mess to be blamed on us. You need to understand the investigation is not over and we don't have all the answers at this point. Because of its sensitive nature, the Lieutenant made you aware of it right away."

He nodded. "It was the right thing to do. We have to get a handle on it before it blows up in our faces. So you guys lay it all out and I'll jump in if Duncan tries to pull any fast ones."

Chapter Forty-Four

Farmingham's Chief of Staff, Debbie Salido, stuck her head around the door, made a show of counting heads, then ducked back out. A moment later Farmingham marched in, followed by Salido, who shut and locked the door behind her.

The supervisor wore a pressed beige pantsuit with a black blouse, accessorized with a necklace with large turquoise stones that looked like it weighed three pounds. Her shoulder length hair was graying but styled to give her a distinguished look. A lined face looked much younger with expertly applied makeup.

Ignoring everyone in the room, she strode to the head of the table and sat. Salido took the chair to her right. Duncan sat on the left side of the table across from the chief and his detectives. Making eye contact with them all, she began speaking.

"We are here today to get to the bottom of a very serious issue. From what I have heard so far, the county is in a very precarious position. We must work together as a team to fix this before the media finds out about it and makes us all look like fools. So it is imperative that you tell me the facts of the case, and hold nothing back, no matter how bad it is. Chief, I assume these are the detectives assigned to the case?"

"Yes, ma'am," he said. "This is Detective Ron Jackson, and Detective Mary Ann McDonald, both veterans of the department. They are the lead investigators and will share their findings. I must caution you, the investigation is far from over, and there are many questions we do not yet have answers to. As soon as they realized the ramifications of the evidence collected, they notified their superior, Lieutenant Warner, who notified me. I felt it critical to contact Director Duncan since the investigation involved his department."

Duncan interrupted. "We don't know that for a fact, Newman. Let's not jump to conclusions."

Farmingham gave him a sharp look, then cleared her throat. "Here are the rules of engagement. We will let the detectives present their findings. I may ask questions. You two—" she pointed at the chief and the director, "—will remain silent unless I ask you a direct question. Detectives, you may proceed."

Ron opened the murder book and laid out their case, point by point. When he needed a break, Mary Ann jumped in. An hour later, they finished their presentation by identifying Natalie Martinez as one of the eight kidnapped children.

Farmingham sat stone-faced at the head of the table. The tension in the room ratcheted up while everyone waited for her to speak. The detectives knew there were too many holes in the investigation, which would raise questions about their competency, and that of the chief.

Her eyes narrowed as she frowned at them. "So this whole thing, starting out as a murder investigation, has morphed into a probable kidnapping by Art Garcia, and probable child trafficking by Angela Garcia, her brother, and maybe Patsy Stonehead. Evidence points to eight kids being kidnapped. One we know is Natalie Martinez.

For the other seven, we don't have names. You do not know where any of them are now. Nor do you know who killed Angela. There is no proof Patsy Stonehead has anything to do with this other than a piece of paper which may or may not contain her initials. You have been working on this case for *seventeen days*, and this is all you have. Does that about cover everything, detectives?" Her voice dripped with contempt.

Chief Newman jumped in. "Ma'am, the investigation is far from over. With more time, I'm confident the detectives can find the answers to these questions."

"Time is something we have precious little of, ladies and gentlemen. These children could be suffering abuses too horrible to dwell on," Farmingham said. "Director Duncan, before we open this for discussion, I want to hear your report."

Roger Duncan, unlike the Chief, served at the discretion of the Board. He could be fired tomorrow by a simple majority vote of the member supervisors.

He sat up as tall as his five-foot-eight height allowed and took a sip of water. "When I became aware *yesterday* of the situation which the detectives have just described, I launched an investigation to find out what we knew about Natalie Martinez."

After a second sip of water, he continued. "When we take responsibility for a child, a case file is created by entering information about the child into the Child Services database. At that point, we assign a caseworker to the case, who handles the child until a relative takes custody, or the court determines the child's fate. If we do not create the file, there will be no record of the child coming into our custody. We searched our records and did not find a case file for Natalie Martinez. Since we did not know she existed, no alarms were raised."

He continued. "If Angela Garcia picked the child up from the police department, and we have only the word of officer Tony Crone for that, it was Ms. Garcia's responsibility to create a case file. I have no idea why she failed to do this. The detectives suggest Ms. Garcia became a rogue employee, selling these kids for her own personal gain. I spoke with her immediate supervisor about her character, and he assured me she was a model employee as long as he knew her. She was his right hand, in charge of the office during his absence."

"Who was her supervisor?" asked Farmingham.

"Ricardo Rodriguez."

Supervisor Farmingham exchanged glances with Salido. "Please go on."

Duncan nodded. "If the detectives' hypothesis is correct, Garcia took a child not once, but eight times. I can't imagine she could do that without someone, somewhere in the county, noticing something amiss."

He got to his point. "Perhaps there is another possibility. Suppose someone else took these kids before Angela ever got them and planted evidence to point the blame at her? Maybe that person killed her to cover it up. The detectives state they have no proof that Patsy Stonehead is a part of this. It seems to me she might have been the one who killed her and stole these kids." He tossed an accusing look at Ron and Mary Ann. "Why haven't you investigated this?"

A moment of silence gripped the room. Ron squeezed the arms of his chair so tightly his knuckles turned white. His face flushed with anger; a snarl came to his lips. Mary Ann kicked him under the table.

Farmingham's voice broke the tension. "Thank you, Director, for your report. To summarize, it is your belief Angela Garcia is an innocent victim. An unknown person, perhaps Patsy Stonehead, took these children, planted the list in the safe, then convinced Tony Crone to put Angela's name into the police database."

Pausing, she made eye contact with Duncan. "I agree with you. It seems impossible Garcia did this eight times without being caught, but it is even more unlikely that the scenario you suggest occurred. There is no evidence to support it. If Stonehead put the list in the safe, why would she put the initials PS on it?"

"Let me ask you some questions, Director Duncan," Farmingham began. "Let's say Angela did in fact pick up Natalie from Sergeant Crone. What prevented her from taking the child to her house instead of back to Child Services?"

"Nothing restrained her from doing that," he replied, "but her moral character would have to be deeply flawed. We have no evidence of that."

"So if she took the child to her house directly from the police station, there would be no record of Natalie anywhere in Child Services, correct?"

"Correct," he agreed.

"And you agree Angela was always the person contacted when Child Services took custody of a child?"

"As far as I'm aware, yes."

"Okay. We have established she was the gatekeeper for any calls from Sergeant Crone and could do what she wanted with the child after taking custody. Is there any other way Ms. Garcia might have gained control over those children?"

Looking miserable, Duncan shifted in his chair.

"There is one other way. Occasionally, the police will discover an abandoned baby. The infant is always sent to Mercy Hospital for a checkup. Once the baby is pronounced healthy, the hospital calls us for a pickup."

"Let me guess," Farmingham moaned. "The person they called was Angela Garcia?"

"Correct," he said, staring up at the ceiling.

"Oh, my Lord. Did she steal babies as well? Chief Newman, are these babies in your database?"

"No," he admitted. "Protocol was always to take the baby to the hospital. We never took formal custody, so we would not have created a record. But the hospital should have records on whom they released the baby to."

Farmingham exploded. "I have never seen anything so screwed up in my entire life. The police database doesn't talk to the child services database, and the hospital database communicates with no one. Garcia steals eight children and no agency has a clue as to what is happening."

When she paused to take a drink of water. Ron noted her hand trembled.

"This is an enormous disaster for the County. If this leaks to the media, it will go viral in less than an hour, and all hell will break loose. Missing babies will make national news. Many people, including some of us in this room, will lose their jobs. We've got to find these kids. It's critical we get into the police database and find names to match those dates in the notebook. We're just running around in the dark without them. Chief, take all the resources you need from Information Services to make it happen."

She turned to her chief of staff. "Debbie, talk to the Director of IS as soon as we're done here. Tell him to give the police department any resources they want. This is the top priority. We need those names today."

"Yes, ma'am," Salido said, taking rapid notes.

"Detectives, get over to the hospital as quickly as possible. See if you can match those dates to any babies in their system. My staff will call the hospital CEO to insure his cooperation. Chief, give your people all the help they want, twenty-four hours a day. I want hourly updates."

"Yes, ma'am."

"Director Duncan, we need a new protocol for taking custody of children. There need to be checks and balances. No more single point of failure. I want recommendations on my desk tomorrow."

"Yes, ma'am."

"Not a word of what we have discussed here shall leave this room. Do not explain to anyone why you need information. If anyone, and I mean anyone, is not cooperative, let me know immediately. Now all of you get the hell out of here."

The chief beckoned to Ron and Mary Ann when they were in the hall. "Leave with me and let's talk outside where it's a little more private."

****

They all piled into the elevator along with Duncan. Nobody said a word on the way down to the first floor. As soon as the elevator doors opened, the director bolted out toward the parking lot without a backward glance. Newman stopped a safe distance from the building and appraised the detectives.

"You two are the best I've got. I'm counting on you to sort this out and solve this case. From now on you report to me. I'll clear it with Warner. Here's my private cell phone number. One of you needs to call me hourly so I can keep Farmingham off my ass. If somebody is not cooperating, call me. Do you need anything right now?"

"We've got enough evidence to arrest Garcia for the kidnapping of Natalie Ramirez," said Ron. "The fingerprints in his van were hers and matched ones from Angela's house. With a warrant, every cop in town will be looking for him. While we're at the hospital, would you establish surveillance on his home?"

The chief nodded. "I'll take care of it. Overtime is not an issue here. I want you guys on this twenty-four-seven."

"You got it, chief," Mary Ann said, and they parted ways.

Chapter Forty-Five

Dennis Korn, CEO for Mercy Hospital was a fit man with curly black hair, a square jaw and a pencil mustache. An impressive Italian wool suit, which likely cost a thousand dollars, completed his appearance. His office was paneled in wood, with one wall containing a large bookcase. The polished mahogany desk with two sidebars that he sat behind dominated the room.

He rose to shake hands with Ron and Mary Ann, then waved them to upholstered red leather easy chairs in front of his desk. His secretary turned to leave, closing the double doors behind her.

He came right to the point. "Detectives, I received a call from Supervisor Farmingham's office this morning that you were coming here on a matter of much urgency. I was asked to assist in any way possible, asking no questions. So let's skip the preliminaries and get right to it. How can I be of help?"

Ron began. "We are investigating a case involving abandoned babies which may have come under your custody. Evidence suggests dates when we believe they were discharged from the hospital. We're trying to research the history of these babies, and the name of the person who took custody of them after discharge. Will your hospital records contain this information?"

Nodding, he picked up his phone. "Amy, find Beth Logan. Ask her to come to my office, please."

His attention returned to the detectives. "Beth is our liaison with the police and Child Services," he said in explanation. "She should have the answers you are searching for."

Ten minutes later, Logan arrived, looking worried and out of breath. He beckoned her in, did the introductions, and told her what the detectives wanted.

She smiled enthusiastically. "If the babies were here, we will have a record of how they got here, who took them, and when they left. I must go back to my office to access the database. Would you detectives like to follow me?"

"Sure, let's go," said Ron.

Chapter Forty-Six

The detectives followed Logan a short distance down another hallway to her office, much more modest than the one they left. It was windowless, with dull white paint on the walls, and a scuffed linoleum floor that needed cleaning. She ushered them to a couple of ordinary straight-backed chairs next to a wall. Composing herself behind her desk, she guided the keyboard toward her fingers. Mary Ann gave her the seven dates on the list in the safe. After a few minutes of typing, she found records for the first three and the sixth on the list, but nothing on the remaining three.

Spinning her wheeled chair around to a file cabinet standing behind her desk, she began thumbing through files, pulling four out of the cabinet, one at a time. With a relieved grin, she placed them on her desk in front of the detectives, announcing, "Everything you want to know should be in these files."

"Excellent," replied Ron. "Before we look at them, can I ask you a few questions?"

"Sure."

"Whom do you get these babies from?"

"Almost always from the police. The babies are typically found during their investigations, and the protocol is to bring them here for examination and evaluation. Once their health needs have been addressed, they are turned over to Child Services."

"Is there someone you routinely call at Child Services when a baby is ready to leave?"

Logan hesitated. "Well, it used to be Angela Garcia, but she died, so I've been calling her supervisor."

"Did she pick up the babies herself, or did someone else?"

"She picked them up about half of the time."

Ron picked up the top file on the desk and began scanning the paperwork. Mary Ann took the next. After a few minutes, he looked up. "Who is Austin Study?"

"My relief. I go home at four, and he works the swing shift. We get kids at all hours, so somebody has to be on call."

Putting down the first file, Ron took another off the stack and began reading it. "Study handled this one, too. Do you know a Christine Ravine?"

"The name sounds familiar."

"The file says she picked up the kid."

"It's possible. There's a lot of staff turnover in Child Services. It might be a new employee I haven't met."

Mary Ann tossed the last file on the desk. "These show the same names; Study and Ravine."

"Excuse me a minute," said Ron. He slipped out into the hall and dialed a number on his cell phone.

"Child Services, Director Duncan's office, Alexis Brown speaking."

"This is Detective Jackson, Santa Barbara Sheriff's Office. I'm calling to verify employment of a Christine Ravine with your department."

"You need to call Human Resources detective. I'm not allowed to give out that information," Brown replied.

"This is a high priority request, and I don't have time to deal with your bureaucracy. If you think I'm kidding, ask your boss what you should do. He's quite familiar with the situation."

"Please hold."

Ron counted to one hundred before she returned. "I searched our records and no one by the name of Christine Ravine has ever worked here," she said.

"Thank you," he said, and broke the connection.

Clipping his phone onto his belt, he reentered Logan's office. "We seem to have an issue here," he said. "Child Services does not have a Christine Ravine working for them."

Logan's face paled. "But...but that's impossible," she stammered. "We made a copy of her ID when she picked up the kids. It's in the files."

They flipped through paper until they found the picture. The quality was poor, a grainy, black and white photocopy. It appeared to be a valid Child Services ID. Neither detective recognized her as Angela Garcia or Patsy Stonehead.

Mary Ann had an idea. "Beth, is there any security camera footage which might show this Christine Ravine?"

Logan, visibly shaken by the possibility of what looked like a huge screw up by the hospital, did not know the answer to this question. She called the head of security and put him on her speakerphone. He asked for the dates they wanted. The latest one was June 2, 2017.

"Ah, that's unfortunate," he said. "We destroy any tapes after six months. Can't keep them forever."

Ron thought of another possibility. "Beth, did you ever meet Ravine?"

She shook her head. "No, she always arrived during Study's shift."

"Is that an unusual coincidence?"

"It's hard to say. The people from Child Services are very busy, but it's more common for them to pick up the babies earlier in the day."

"Did you know Angela Garcia personally?"

"Oh yes, I knew her well."

"Did Austin Study ever meet her?"

"I…I'm not sure. Would you like me to ask him?"

He nodded.

She consulted her address book, picked up her phone, and dialed a number, again putting the call on speakerphone. Study answered on the second ring. Logan introduced the detectives, passing the questioning over to them.

"Mr. Study, do you know a Christine Ravine from Child Services?" asked Ron.

"Yes, I do," Study replied. "Why?"

"Did she meet with you to take custody of four babies?"

"I don't recall an exact number but hospital records would show the dates and times."

"Did you ever meet or talk to her before that time?"

"No."

"How were you notified she was coming to pick up a baby?"

"Beth would leave me a note if turnover hadn't occurred by the end of her shift."

Logan broke in. "That's where I recognize the name! If Angela couldn't make it, she'd call to say Ravine would do the pickup."

Ron nodded and resumed his questioning of Study. "Do you know Angela Garcia?"

"I may have talked to her at some point, but I don't

believe I ever met her."

"Anything that seemed at all strange to you during your time with Ravine? Did she seem nervous or say something odd?"

There was a pause while Study considered it. "No..." he said finally. "A little impatient to get the paperwork done, but she always got here kind of late in the day, so I thought nothing of it. She claimed to have only been with Child Services about four months."

"Thank you for your time, Mr. Study. Please do not discuss this with anyone else. This is an open investigation, and we don't want to tip anyone off who might be a suspect."

"Oh, sure. No problem," agreed Study.

Logan disconnected the call.

"If it's not too much trouble," Ron asked, "would you make us copies of each of these files to take with us?"

"Sure thing."

While she took the files over to the photocopier, he looked over at his partner and raised an eyebrow. Mary Ann shrugged. Nothing left to discover at Mercy Hospital.

Chapter Forty-Seven

On the drive back to the office, Ron called the chief to fill him in.

"Got to find out who this Ravine is," Newman said. "Use the new facial recognition software and run her picture against the mug shots. It should be able to find a match. I'll have a tech standing by to assist you. I've told Information Services to get our database to search by date. They said the software is so old nobody knows how to program it. Do you believe that shit? I told them I need it done by tomorrow or somebody is going to be looking for a new job. I've got no time to baby those nerds. Keep me updated."

His phone clicked dead. Ron glowered at Mary Ann. "What?" she said.

"The chief's trying to run our investigation. He wants us to search mug shots using facial recognition software to find out who Christine Ravine is. I already know in my gut it's Angela Garcia. Instead of wasting time running mug shots, I'm just going to give the tech a picture of Angela and see if they match."

She nodded. "No argument from me. I think it's her too—or Stonehead. Did you notice the four dates the hospital found all carried the letters 'PS'?"

"Yeah, I did. So that might explain why Angela did business with both her brother and Stonehead. Patsy specialized in babies, and Art took the older kids."

"Seems kind of weird to me," she replied. "Why wouldn't one or the other just take any kid? Why the need for both of them?"

He shook his head but said nothing. Mary Ann turned left into the office driveway and swung the car around back to park. They entered through the back door.

The vibe inside the station was different. It got quiet when the detectives entered, and everyone avoided eye contact as they walked to their desks. The grapevine had spread the word they were working on something very heavy, having to do with the Angela Garcia case, and involving cops. Tony Crone had shared with his buddies the fact Mary Ann asked him questions about the case, too. As a result, the natural paranoia which exists in every police force grew like a weed. Everyone would steer clear of them until it was determined whatever was going on didn't involve them. As Ron predicted, they were now pariahs.

"I'll bet we've got the LT pissed off at us," Mary Ann said. "He thinks we requested to report to the chief."

Ron blew out a breath. "Now everybody hates us."

He sat down, placing a bag containing lunch on his desk. They had passed by a drive thru on the way back to the office. The smell of hot French fries rose from the bag, making him even hungrier. The message waiting lamps on the detective's phones blinked furiously.

His stomach growled as he debated eating or returning phone calls. "I guess I'd better find out how many death threats I've gotten so far," he told Mary Ann with a sigh.

He listened to more than several messages, the most recent from the department's facial recognition expert who sounded frantic to help.

Must have gotten an earful from his boss.

The second message, from a Corporal Wilson, said he was assigned to tail Art Garcia but couldn't locate him. He was staking out his house, since he didn't have any other idea where to look. If the detective had any suggestions, please call. The last message was a rather chilly one from the LT. Until further notice, Ron would report to the chief on all matters pertaining to the Angela Garcia investigation.

He called the facial recognition tech, who answered immediately, as though he was staring at the phone, waiting for it to ring. He told Ron he'd been assigned to work with both him and Mary Ann; anything they wanted done would take priority.

"Here's what I need," Ron said. "I've got two pictures to send to you. I need to know if they are the same person."

"No problem. I can have it within the hour."

Ron erased names before sending the picture of Angela he copied from her ID badge, and the picture of Christine Ravine he copied from the hospital file. The tech didn't need names to determine if they were the same person.

His phone rang forty-five minutes later as he finished his lunch. The results of the facial recognition analysis showed a ninety percent chance the two pictures matched. The tech said this would stand up in court any day. They never got a one hundred percent probability.

Ron asked him to run Ravine's picture against the mug shots in the database to see if there were any better matches. He didn't expect to find anything, but he didn't want any trouble with the chief either.

They had solid proof Angela Garcia was Christine

Ravine. Despite his frustration, Ron grudgingly respected her accomplishments. She entered a hospital multiple times where many people knew her and left with four babies. Few would have the guts to do it.

Information Services called with an update. They continued working to add the search by date feature to the police database. It was proving to be more difficult than they expected. An all-nighter was planned, and they hoped to have it fixed by morning.

Ron was glad he didn't work in that department, but he knew all the pressure would shift to him once he had names. And there was the problem. Even with names, there was no trail to follow. When Christine Ravine walked out the front door of the hospital, the babies simply disappeared. The detectives would hit the same dead end they had with Natalie Ramirez.

Ron was forced to admit nothing of great importance happened at the hospital. There was no proof Angela turned the babies over to Stonehead or her brother, and no clues about what happened to them. Art Garcia was the only one who could provide answers. And right now, no one knew where he was.

Chapter Forty-Eight

January 27th

"You two look like hell," the LT said, shutting the door to his office. "I won't ask about the case since I'm now out of the loop, but did you look at the paper this morning?"

Not a good way to start the day. With a sinking feeling in his gut, Ron glanced at Mary Ann, who shrugged.

Warner picked up his copy of the Santa Barbara Enquirer and tossed it across his desk. The lead story indicated reliable sources confirmed the police had issued an arrest warrant for Art Garcia, wanted for kidnapping thirteen-year-old Natalie Ramirez. The article noted he was also the brother of Angela Garcia, murdered earlier in January and still the subject of an open investigation by the police.

From there, the reporter strayed from the facts into speculation about Angela being killed by her brother to cover up her involvement in the kidnapping. She handled the welfare of children placed in her care, as she worked for Child Services at the time of her murder.

Child Services had no comment when asked if Natalie Ramirez was in Angela's care at the time she disappeared. A spokesperson for Chief Newman said the police department would have no comment on an active case. The reporter had part of the story, getting dangerously close to the truth, but stonewalled by the county. No mention of seven other children being kidnapped.

Ron sighed. "It could have been worse."

The LT nodded. "Yeah, they didn't put it all together yet. But now it's out there, and those reporters are going to be tripping all over themselves to find out what's going on. They all have sources, and leaks will occur. I just wanted to be sure you two heard about it before the chief calls."

"Thanks, LT. Just for the record, it wasn't our idea to keep you out of the loop on this," Mary Ann declared.

Warner grimaced. "I'm aware of that. They're trying to compartmentalize this to save their own asses if this goes bad. Watch your backs out there. Document everything you do because they'll throw you under the bus in a heartbeat."

The detectives shuffled dispiritedly back to their desks. As though on cue, Ron's cell phone buzzed.

"Did you see the paper this morning?" the chief asked.

"Yes sir, just now."

"Those sons of bitches found out about the warrant and ran with it. Now Farmingham is all over my ass. We've got to find Garcia and wrap this up before the media figures it all out. I put a BOLO on him last night and not a nibble. You and Mary Ann chase down any lead you can find on him. He's your top priority today. When you find him, call for backup. We need him alive or we're screwed, understand?"

The detective remained silent, so he continued. "The IS crew should have the software fixed so we can get the names of the other kids in the database this morning. I told them to call you. You got anything new?"

Ron wanted to point out he just got to work fifteen minutes ago but thought better of it. "No sir."

"All right then. I'm counting on you to find Garcia today." The phone clicked dead.

Ron glared up at the ceiling, trying to control his anger. He felt pain in his left hand, looked down, and found his knuckles were white from holding his cell phone too tightly. He forced his fingers to relax and put the phone down on his desk.

"What?" Mary Ann asked.

"The chief has decreed we are to find Garcia today. He thinks he might have skipped, but we need to find him even if he's in Argentina. Otherwise it's our asses. So get your crystal ball out and tell me where he is."

She made a steeple with her two hands, placed them on her forehead, and closed her eyes. "I'm getting something here...not Argentina...I think Cuba."

"Perfect. While we're there, we can claim political asylum."

Chapter Forty-Nine

Ron checked in with Corporal Wilson, who had just relieved the officer who watched Garcia's house the previous night. The officer reported that no one had visited. The only other activity was a dog sleeping in the front yard that hadn't eaten in a day.

Mary Ann called the duty officer to see who was watching Stonehead's house, and was informed it was Tina Alvarado, a friend of hers.

She called her number. "Tina, are you doing surveillance on Stonehead right now?"

"Yeah, I got the assignment this morning and started watching the house about half an hour ago. No one was available to watch it last night. The house looks empty to me. I've seen nothing except the birds singing. It's possible she left for work before I got here. I'm going to give it another thirty minutes, then cruise by her office to see if I can pick up her trail there."

Mary Ann thanked her, told her to keep in touch, and relayed the information to her partner.

"Wonderful," Ron grumbled. "Not only don't we know where Garcia is, but now we don't have a clue where Stonehead is, either. Something's going on; I feel it in my bones."

Before she could reply, Jack Liu, from Information Services, called Ron.

"Hey Jack, how's it going?"

"It took all night to figure out that damn obsolete code nobody knows anymore, but we did it." Liu sounded both exhausted and excited. "I've got names on three kids: Daniel Turner, Abigail Montenegro, and William Mendoza. Our records say they were all picked up by Angela Garcia. None have any juvenile records. Child Services might have something, but you'd have to ask them. We don't have access to their database."

"Thanks Jack, that's outstanding work. Go get some sleep. We'll take it from here."

As he hung up, Ron felt the monkey jump off of Liu's back and onto his own. The ball was now in his court and the chief wanted results ASAP.

His next call was to Child Services. After he identified himself to Duncan's secretary, she transferred the call to the great man himself without delay.

"What is it, detective?" He sounded annoyed.

"Director, we have identified the names of an additional three children on Angela Garcia's list. I'm requesting that you check your database for any information you might have on them."

There was a slight pause on the line. "Give me the names. I'll have them checked out," he snapped.

Next, Ron called the chief to brief him on the latest developments.

"So all you got are three names?" Newman said, sounding disappointed.

"Yes, sir. I gave the names to Director Duncan. He is currently searching his records to determine what information Child Services has on them."

"I'll bet you he finds nothing. Angela Garcia was twice as smart as that idiot. Keep me informed."

Ron hung up and turned to compare notes with Mary Ann, but she was on her phone. He finished his coffee, and was debating getting a refill, when she slammed down the phone, looking worried.

"What?" he said.

"That call was from a Cindy Thompson, who is quite concerned about the whereabouts of her boss. She had a date to be in court at nine a.m. this morning and didn't show. The judge's clerk called Thompson to complain about the no show. She hadn't heard from her boss, so she tried all the numbers she had to find her but got nowhere. The boss left instructions to call me if this happened. She was afraid of a man who she said might try to kill her."

Puzzled and more than a little impatient, Ron asked, "What's this got to do with our case?"

"Her boss is Patsy Stonehead."

"Ah shit."

Chapter Fifty

Mary Ann placed a quick call back to Tina Alvarado. "Stonehead's reported missing. I need you to ring her doorbell to see if she's there. If she doesn't answer, do an exterior inspection to check for forced entry. Call me back, ASAP."

The detectives waited, the tension rising with every passing minute. Twenty minutes later, Alvarado called back. "I got no response when I rang the doorbell, so I did a walk around. At the back I found a French door with a pane of glass busted out, possible forced entry. I'm returning to my patrol car so I can watch the front of the house."

"Okay, maintain your position. We're on our way."

They raced out the back door of the station and piled into their car. Ron drove, siren wailing, while Mary Ann called the chief to inform him Stonehead was missing and of a possible forced entry at her home. Newman swore a blue streak for a few minutes, finally calming down enough to tell her to call him when they got there.

The tension in the car ratcheted up another notch. After the thirty-minute drive, they screeched to a halt in front of Stonehead's house and were greeted by Alvarado. "See anything else?" Mary Ann asked.

"Nothing at all. Been real quiet, no locals around."

Ron laid out their plan. "We'll head around to the back and gain entry to the house through the French door. Tina, we need you to watch the front in case somebody tries to leave while we're in there. We'll call you when we finish. Then, we'll go from there."

Alvarado nodded and took a position behind her patrol car parked at the curb. Drawing their weapons, the detectives headed around the side of the house, following a sidewalk leading through a gate to the backyard. Ron peered around the corner, saw nothing suspicious in the backyard, and inched forward. Mary Ann positioned herself behind and to his right side, away from the house, so she would have a clear line of fire. They passed two windows, both with curtains closed on their way to the French door, which was under a covered patio containing a table and chairs.

A raven, sitting on a low branch in a maple tree in the backyard, screeched at them. Ron remembered ravens were bad omens, symbols of death. *Was there a dead person in the house or was his own death being foretold by the bird?*

He crept on toward the door, trying to ignore the bird. It fixed an eye on him, following his progress, making him even more nervous.

Small pebbles of safety glass were scattered around on the ground below a missing windowpane in the French door. He glanced back at his partner, who nodded that she was ready. Ron used his left hand to try turning the doorknob, but found it locked. Carefully stretching his hand through the missing pane, he turned the doorknob from inside until the door gave inward when he pushed against it.

"Police!" he shouted and swung the door open.

Met with silence, he motioned for Mary Ann to go right. He took a defensive stance and stepped through the door, hurrying to his left. Dim light filtered in from the open French door. A large dining room table and chairs dominated the room.

"Police!" he shouted again. "Come out now with your hands up!"

More silence. He felt a sinister presence in the house like something very evil waited. They glided forward, careful to make no sound. Two doorways branched off the hallway, one led into the kitchen and the other into a room around the corner from where they stood. Ron inched along the wall toward the unseen room, while Mary Ann covered the doorway to the kitchen. Sweat trickled down his neck as he peeked quickly into the other room. The lights were off, and the drapes drawn, allowing only a sliver of daylight to penetrate. Two chairs sat in the middle of the room, where they didn't belong. One was empty. In the shadowed light he saw a shapeless lump in the other.

"I might have something here," he whispered.

Mary Ann moved over to the other side of the doorway and took a peek. "Something in the chair."

Ron took another look and noticed a light switch on the wall near him. "I'm going to switch on the lights. Be ready." He slid his left hand around the corner and flipped on the switch. A lamp in the room's corner lit up.

"Oh Jesus."

His shaking hands forced him to lower his gun toward the floor in case it discharged accidentally. At his side, Mary Ann gasped in horror, retreated into the dining room, back peddled into a wall and slid down to the floor.

Chapter Fifty-One

The chair contained the body of a naked woman. Multiple stab wounds covered her torso, indicating torture. Her legs had been taped to the chair, both hands bound behind her back. Her head rested on her chest, looking downward. A knife protruded from her left eye socket. The eyeball dangled from a thin piece of tissue on her cheek.

Ron forced himself to walk over to see the full face of the dead woman. It was Patsy Stonehead. The detectives took a few minutes to settle their nerves before searching the rest of the house. None of the other rooms appeared to be touched. Ron called the chief to tell him what they found.

"Son of a bitch!" he shouted. "That goddamn Garcia did it. He's killing all the witnesses to save his ass. I'll get a team out there to handle the crime scene right now. As soon as they get there, give your statements, then get back on him. Don't tell them anything about Stonehead being tied into this case."

"The airlines, railroad, bus, and rental car companies checked their records this morning and Garcia booked nothing. He's still in town or took off in his car. If he skipped, I want confirmation, you understand?"

"Yes, sir," Ron said, aware there was a third possibility. "Could we get the surveillance tapes from all the transportation companies for the last twenty-four hours? He might have used a disguise and fake identity to book a trip. We can use the facial recognition software to confirm that."

Newman considered the request. "Yeah, okay, it wouldn't hurt," he admitted. "I'll take care of it. You guys stay on his tail."

Ron put his phone away, noticing the tremor in his hands. He didn't think he would ever get the picture of Stonehead with a knife in her eye out of his head.

"The chief is sending out a team," he informed Mary Ann. "He wants us back on Garcia as soon as they get here."

"We don't have any idea where he is," she replied.

He remembered to call Alvarado. "Stonehead's dead. The house is empty. Tape off the property line and wait for the crime team to show up."

The detectives went back to the murder scene, looking for clues. The victim had been gagged with her own panties. Her face was bruised and swollen, her broken nose bent to the side. Ron counted at least ten stab wounds on her body. The duct tape binding her hands and feet, had a shiny look to it, similar to the tape found in the back of Garcia's van. The victim's shredded clothes lay scattered around on the floor by her chair. A bloody pillowcase was nearby. Whoever killed her did so in a blind rage.

In the kitchen, they found small drops of blood splattered around the sink.

"This might be the suspect's blood," Ron said. "Maybe there was a struggle and Stonehead scratched him before he subdued her."

In the utility room, Mary Ann found a purse on the

floor. "Looks like he surprised her when she arrived home from work, tied her up, and tortured her. If it was Garcia, what did she have that he wanted?"

"Maybe he wanted to know how she fit into the kidnapping business with Angela," replied Ron. "He needed to make sure there were no loose ends that could come back on him. Stonehead might have been less than forthcoming with her answers, and the interrogation got out of hand. Or it could be a case of revenge for getting screwed out of Angela's property. So he kills her last night, gets away early before surveillance gets established by Alvarado, and goes where?"

"It would have to be somewhere he feels safe," answered Mary Ann. "He must know by now there's a warrant out for his arrest. Can't risk driving around in his own car. So either he has a safe house where he's holed up or he rabbited somewhere else."

"Did he strike you as an intelligent guy?" asked Ron. "Someone who would have a plan if something like this happened?"

"No. He struck me as a blue-collar type. Somebody living day to day, making enough to scratch out a living, not worrying too much about the future."

"Exactly. He's got to be headed home. It's his only place of refuge. There might be a way to get inside without being seen from the road. As soon as we're done here, let's pay a visit."

She shrugged. "Is there a chance somebody else killed Stonehead for something that has nothing to do with Garcia?"

His brow furrowed. "Anything's possible, but that duct tape looked like the roll I saw in his van."

The crime scene team showed up in record time.

Nothing like a call from the chief to get some action. Two detectives from the station, Mason and Staller, arrived separately. Ron and Mary Ann exchanged greetings and then gave their statements. Mason asked why they weren't taking the case.

"We're on a special assignment on orders of the chief. He doesn't want us bogged down in another case."

Nodding, Mason took the hint and asked no more questions. The detectives rushed to their car.

Chapter Fifty-Two

Art drove the back roads to avoid detection, when the all-news channel on his radio announced he was the subject of an arrest warrant issued for the kidnapping of Natalie Ramirez.

That's nothing. Wait until they find Stonehead.

His memory contained gaps about what had happened. He lost his sanity and did horrible things to the woman; he knew that, but the details eluded him. Perhaps his mind was protecting him from the horror. All the frustration, the betrayal, the unfairness of it all had come boiling to the surface. The bitch lied to him multiple times about her business with Angela, and that pushed him over the edge. He hadn't gone there to kill her, but he warned her what would happen if she lied, so she got what she deserved.

Now he knew all of Patsy Stonehead's secrets. He also had the complete picture of the hidden life his sister led, and he harbored no more guilt for her death. That cold, self-centered bitch got what she deserved, too.

He drove to his storage unit, rented under a fake name, and packed his remaining drugs into the trunk of his car. He kept extra clothes there for emergencies, so he changed out of his blood-soaked shirt and pants.

Time to rest for a while, as his next stop was the bank, which would not be open until eight o'clock. He backed his car into the storage unit, took a quick look around, and lowered the roll-up door. Crawling into the backseat, he fell into a sleep of exhaustion until eight a.m., when the alarm on his phone woke him.

Again, he took the side streets, less chance of being seen by patrolling cops. Shortly before nine, he arrived at his bank. The lobby was crowded with customers, so no one paid him any attention. After filling out the required paperwork, a clerk took him to the back of the bank where the safe deposit boxes were stacked in the vault.

Alone in a room with his box, he held the ticket in his hands for the last time. Coming back here again would be too risky with every cop in the county looking for him. He imagined collecting the money, and the lifestyle it would make possible. Lavish vacations, exotic cars, a mansion in the most expensive area of Santa Barbara. It should all have been his.

Yanking himself back to the present, he shook his head angrily. His fate was cast. No point in pretending otherwise. He would try to sneak into his house, gather his guns and money, and make a run for it. He figured his chances of getting away at close to zero. If the cops cornered him, he had a backup plan, and he was at peace with it.

Dropping one more item he brought from Stonehead's house into the box, he called for the teller, and watched her lock it up. If he couldn't cash the ticket, no one else would either.

He left the bank, gazing down at the floor to avoid the security cameras getting a good look at him. Driving to his house would not be easy. Only one way to get there, straight up the 101 freeway. With an arrest warrant against him, every cop in the county would be looking for his car. It was a matter of luck if he made it without being stopped.

On the drive up, he passed a Highway Patrol cop busy writing a speeding ticket to a motorist, paying no attention to the passing traffic. When he could no longer see the officer in his rear-view mirror, he grinned. So far, his luck held.

Certain his house was being watched, he planned to enter from the rear. A dirt trail on his neighbor's property, used to check on his cattle, ran for a short distance near the back boundary of Garcia's property. The trail would get him close, then he could sneak into the house on foot through the backyard. Collecting his money and guns would take only twenty minutes. He would leave the way he came in, and no one would be the wiser.

****

As his car bounced along the rutted trail, Art checked the rear-view mirror, driving slowly, leaving no cloud of dust behind him. His car creaked and groaned as it passed over potholes and rocks. The trail ran below a ridge, blocking anyone observing the front of his house from seeing him. When he reached the point where the trail was closest to his property, he swung his car around to face the direction he came from and killed the motor.

He remained still for a moment, then crawled up the ridge on his belly to survey the back of his house, alert for any movement. In front of him, a barbed wire fence delineated his property line. He would have to climb over it, then dash across open ground for another thirty feet to his back door. Not a speck of cover anywhere, which was how he planned it, as a defense against intruders. Now it was proving to be a disadvantage.

He planned to stay behind his house and enter through the back door. The house would block anyone watching the front from seeing him. But a cop stationed further up in the woods along the border of his property would spot him in a second, and he would never make it to the door.

He debated the odds, deciding out of desperation it was worth the chance. Without his money, he had nothing to live on or rebuild his business, and he needed his guns for protection.

Slithering over the ridgeline, he sprinted down to the fence. Picking a spot between two sturdy wood posts, he leaned all his weight on the wire. It bowed but did not break. Encouraged, he threw his knapsack over the fence, placed both hands on the wire between the barbs, and sprang high, vaulting himself over it. He cleared the wire with inches to spare and fell to the ground on the other side.

Wasting no time, he ran, crouched over, to the back door. No cops in the woods challenged him, so his luck continued to hold. He congratulated himself on his undetected approach, then frowned as his dog rushed around the side of the house, whining with excitement. Apparently, he hadn't been as quiet as he thought. A few pats on the dog's head calmed him down.

Quickly unlocking the back door, he slipped inside, with the dog on his heels. He deactivated the inside security alarms and peeked out a crack in the curtains covering the front window. He saw nothing that didn't belong there. Satisfied he made it safely inside, he activated all his exterior alarms, making sure everything worked properly.

The dog scratched at the cabinet that held his food

in the kitchen, and he realized, with a pang of guilt, it hadn't eaten in over a day. Although time was precious, he retrieved a bag of dog food from the pantry and dumped it on the floor. The dog would have to stay behind, so this would give him enough to eat until someone found him. The kitchen clock hanging over the sink told him he had already been in the house for ten minutes. He hurried into his bedroom to pack.

Chapter Fifty-Three

After leaving the carnage at Stonehead's home, the detectives drove North up the 101 toward Santa Maria. Ron felt depressed, the case had spiraled out of his control. He failed to protect Stonehead, perhaps the only person other than Garcia who could help them. If surveillance had been established earlier, she might still be alive. He had only a faint hope of finding Garcia at home. If that didn't pan out, he would be left twisting in the wind with no more leads to follow other than a search of Patsy's home. The pressure from the chief and Farmingham would be unbearable. They might decide to pull him off the case in disgrace.

During the entire investigation, he felt he'd been one step behind. He considered this the biggest case of his career, and he was failing miserably. Maybe he didn't have what it took to be a detective any longer.

It was early afternoon, and because of the Stonehead investigation, they were hours behind schedule. Ron turned the police flashers on and pushed the car close to ninety. His phone rang as they flashed by the town of Buellton. Duncan's secretary calling, to tell him Child Services had no record of the other three kids Ron had given her boss.

After relaying the information to Mary Ann, she said, "I guess we got lucky on the one kid old enough to have a prior record."

"Yeah, without that we wouldn't have anything. Angela made a mistake when she grabbed Natalie Martinez without checking first to see if she had a record."

"She forgot about fingerprints, too."

Thirty minutes later, they arrived in Santa Maria, easing up behind Corporal Wilson's car, on a patch of dirt about a quarter mile from Garcia's house. They all gathered by the side of the road to confer.

"We're in a bind," said Ron. "There was a homicide last night. Might involve Garcia, but we can't find him anywhere. A warrant's out, and every cop in Santa Barbara County is searching for him. He's desperate, and somebody else is going to get hurt if we don't find him soon. Hoped he might come back here since we have no intelligence, he has anywhere else to go."

Wilson, a barrel-chested man with a handlebar mustache, scratched his chin.

"I've been here since seven and the only thing that's moved up there is the dog. The best way for him to sneak in would be from the back, but he wouldn't be able to drive his car back in there. There're no roads, it's cattle country. He'd have to hike in. Be impossible for him to make a quick getaway. If I was him, I'd wait until night to try it, and then get out before dawn."

"Can you see the backyard at all from here?" asked Mary Ann.

"No," he responded. "If I got any closer, he'd spot me pretty quick. I use binoculars to check the front."

"Can I look?" asked Ron.

"Sure, let me get them out of the car."

After Wilson handed a pair of high-powered binoculars to Ron, he swept the front of the house.

"You say the dog's up there?"

"Yep, he stays in the front yard probably hoping somebody will come by and feed him."

He scanned the house again. "I don't see the dog."

"Let me look," replied Wilson. He raised the binoculars to scan the house. "He was up there about fifteen minutes ago. Probably ran around to the back for something." He realized what he said. "Son of a bitch, Garcia came in the back way and the dog heard him."

"We'd better go check out the house," Ron said. "If the dog doesn't come to meet us, it's in the house, which means Garcia is in there too. Wilson, can you work your way around to cover the back if he makes a run for it?"

Wilson scanned the terrain. "I can cut up through those woods on the left and get into position in about fifteen minutes."

"Okay, you do that, and call us on the radio when you're set. Then we'll drive up to the front and see if the dog comes. If we confirm Garcia's in there, we'll back off and call for backup."

He nodded, hastened to his car to retrieve his shotgun, jogged across the road, and disappeared into the woods. The detectives returned to their car to await his signal.

"We might be a driving into an ambush," said Mary Ann. "We're not heavily armed."

They had only their service pistols with them.

"I'm going to be real careful driving up there. I'll stop in the driveway and see if the dog comes. If not, I'll see if we can bluff him into surrendering."

Their radios squawked to life. "In position."

Ron started the car and drove forward, past the front lawn. He turned left onto the driveway and stopped about halfway to the house. He kept the motor running, lowered his window, and whistled for the dog.

After a short delay, the dog bounded around the corner of the house, coming towards him with his tail wagging. Ron sighed in disappointment. The dog must have chased a squirrel or something around back.

His radio crackled. "Somebody opened the back door and let the dog out. I didn't get a good look at him," Wilson said.

"Copy that," said Ron. "Maintain your position; I'm going to talk him into giving up."

He backed his car further down the driveway toward the street, stopped, opened the car door, and took cover behind it. Mary Ann called in for backup, slid out her door, and took a defensive position behind the right front wheel of the car, with her pistol drawn.

He shouted up to the house. "Art Garcia, this is the police. We have a warrant for your arrest. The house is surrounded. Come out the front door slowly with your hands up."

Chapter Fifty-Four

The alarms started going off as soon as the invisible motion sensor across the driveway was broken. Rushing into the room housing his surveillance monitors, Garcia saw an unmarked car with two people in it coming up the driveway. It stopped before getting to the house. The driver's window rolled down and Ron Jackson's head became visible.

Jackson began whistling. This puzzled Garcia until he noticed the dog's ears perk up and his head turn towards the living room. He quickly grabbed the dog's collar, took him into the bathroom, and closed the door. Why had he let the dog inside? He cursed himself for his stupidity. Time had run out. He needed to leave now to have any chance of avoiding detection.

His bag waited in the hall. He ran to the back door and peered out the window. If there were cops out front, there might be cops out back, too. If so, the game was over. He saw nothing suspicious in the yard, but the wooded area to the side of his property provided excellent cover. A squad of cops might be in there. There was a thirty-yard sprint with no cover through his backyard to the fence, and then a stop to climb over the barbed wire. He didn't like his odds.

An idea occurred to him. Rushing to the bathroom, he grabbed Mick's collar and led him to the back door. He opened the door a crack and shoved the dog outside.

Jackson whistled in the front yard.

He watched his monitors as the dog bounded around the corner, Jackson's head disappeared back inside the car, and the detectives backed slowly down the driveway. He congratulated himself. The ruse had worked, and they were leaving. Then the car stopped.

Jackson got out of the car and demanded his surrender. The smile disappeared from his face. The dog hadn't fooled them. Or maybe it's a bluff, to get him to reveal himself. If so, there might not be any cops guarding the backyard. It was his last chance to escape. Hoisting his bag over his shoulder, he rushed to the back door, and opened it. Taking one step outside, he froze.

A voice shouted from the woods. "Police! Stop right there. Put your hands up where I can see them. Now!"

He glanced toward the sound of the voice and saw a shadowy figure behind a tree trunk, aiming a shotgun at him. Instead of throwing up his hands, he dived back into the house, slamming the door shut. He rushed back to the surveillance monitors. Jackson was still there in the driveway, talking into a radio, most likely getting a report from the cop in the woodlands. *So this is it*. No way out; either surrender and spend the rest of my life in jail or die.

He unzipped his bag and took out his guns. He loaded the shotgun with slugs, figuring a solid piece of metal would have a better chance of penetrating the car than buckshot. A couch dragged under the front window gave him more protection against return fire. He slammed a magazine into his rifle, cocked it, and placed it on the floor next to him. Taking a deep breath, he was stoic, ready to die.

Chapter Fifty-Five

To the rear of the house, Bob Hackman lay prone, peering over the ridgeline with a pair of binoculars. He was growing increasingly concerned about the events taking place below. After he reported Art's difficulties with the cops to his employer, he received orders to quietly make him disappear. The man knew way too much about Teddy Bear Fantasies that could be shared with the cops if he was arrested.

To make his job easier, he had placed a tracking device on Garcia's vehicle, allowing him to follow his movements. Despite tracking him for days, the opportunity to make him disappear didn't happen. His backup plan was a pound of C-4 explosive with a radio-controlled trigger, placed under the house when unoccupied. A temporary power outage disabled the cameras, and a juicy steak bone kept the dog happy while he worked.

Bob was in a quandary. The event had escalated from a simple grab and run to a shootout. His plan to intercept Garcia after he left the house would not be possible now. The cops had certainly called for backup, so more reinforcements would be arriving shortly. Art might be killed in the shootout, but what if he was only wounded and taken alive or surrendered? That was an unacceptable risk.

He raised his binoculars once more to study the

situation. The cops had stopped far down the driveway, somewhat protected behind their car. Could they survive the explosion? What about the one in the woods, protected by only a tree? If any of them died, it would set off an intense search for him.

There was no more time to debate the issue. A decision needed to be made, before anyone else arrived.

Chapter Fifty-Six

Ron heard sirens coming from far away. *Backup is coming. We'll keep Garcia trapped in the house until they get here.*

Suddenly, he heard the crash of glass breaking. As he looked up at the house, the barrel of a shotgun appeared where the pane of glass had been.

"Gun! Take cover!" he screamed at Mary Ann as he crouched behind the car door.

The roar of the shotgun cut off his words. Something heavy smashed into the side of the car just in front of his door. He checked for damage inside the car and saw a mangled mass of metal near the break petal. Only one type of round could have penetrated that far.

"Holy shit!" he shouted as he dove into the car, crawled across the seat and fell out the passenger side onto the dirt in back of his partner. "He's shooting slugs. Stay behind the wheel."

Another round tore into the front of the car but was stopped by the motor. The radio squawked to life. Wilson wanted to know what was happening.

"Garcia's shooting slugs from the house," Ron said. "We've taken cover behind the car."

"I can come around the side, see if I can get a shot."

"Negative, maintain your position. I don't want him to slip out the back. We'll wait him out until backup arrives."

The detectives had yet to fire a shot while huddled behind the wheel of the car. Another round shattered the front windshield and whistled over Ron's head. He scanned the terrain, searching for a safer place to retreat.

A sudden flash of light lit the sky, followed a second later by the sound of an explosion. The entire house lifted in the air in what seemed like slow motion and blew out in all directions. A giant pressure wave struck the detectives, knocking them back from the car. Dazed, Ron looked for Mary Ann, spotting her lying motionless several feet away. He crawled towards her, intending to shield her from the falling debris. Halfway there, something heavy fell on the back of his head, knocking him out.

In the woods, the pressure wave threw Wilson backwards twenty feet, where he smacked against a tree trunk. The last thing he remembered was sliding to the ground.

Chapter Fifty-Seven

Bob Hackman huddled behind the ridge, waiting for flying debris to settle before crawling out to observe the damage. A smoking crater stood where the house had been. Pieces of splintered wood and asphalt shingles littered the ground. Small fires burned around the yard. No one inside the house could have survived. A destroyed police car sat on its side in the driveway, one wheel spinning in the air. The garage suffered minor damage, a tribute to its solid construction. He did not see the detectives or the cop in the woods.

He blamed himself for causing such a large explosion. The cops might very well be dead, which would subject him to a massive manhunt. He'd guessed at the amount of C-4 needed to do the job, having no previous experience with blowing up a house. A pound was a bit too much.

The sirens grew louder. He needed to be gone before they arrived. His motorcycle stood by, ready to go. Firing up the engine, he took off down the dirt track, back towards the road.

Later today, he would abandon the motorcycle, setting it on fire to destroy any trace evidence. His orders were to leave California.

****

Four minutes later the SWAT team arrived, stunned by the destruction. No one greeted them, and nothing moved. The house was scattered in pieces up to half a mile away. Smoke and dust hung in the air, making it difficult to breathe.

A frantic search and rescue operation began, to find anyone still alive. Fifteen minutes later, while clearing away debris around the destroyed car, a searcher found the unconscious detectives.

It took longer to find Wilson in the woods.

Chapter Fifty-Eight

All three of the officers injured during the "Garcia shootout," as it became known in the media, were transported by Med-Evac choppers to Mercy Hospital. Ron woke up the next day with the worst headache he'd ever had, and a gash on the back of his head that had required thirty stitches. A severe case of tinnitus would last for months.

While recuperating at home, he received a call from the chief. "Ron, I wanted to congratulate you on a job well done. It's a shame we couldn't take that son-of-a-bitch alive, but at least he's not out there preying on kids any longer. How's your head?"

"I'm getting better, sir. Still got the ringing in my ears."

"The doctors say that should go away. I saw the size of that crater. You are damn lucky that explosion didn't kill you. But let's talk about your future. I'm recommending you for a staff job, liaison to the Board of Supervisors. Farmingham requested you. She liked the way you handled the case. You can start as soon as you feel like coming back."

"What about the case, chief? We've still got eight missing kids out there and Angela Garcia's murder to solve."

He cleared his throat. "I considered that, but there's nobody left alive who can help us. You've got no leads.

256

Farmingham's making sure something like this will never happen again. Duncan's leaving, Rodriguez is being reassigned, and we're modernizing the computer systems. It's a terrible thing that happened, but we have to move on."

"Move on? I can't do that, Chief. Let me keep digging. There are other people involved in this, and I want to put them in jail. If we don't do something, they'll just find someone else to provide the kids."

"Ron, listen to me. It's not in anyone's interest to pursue this. You did the best work possible. Everyone recognizes that. You can have a lot of influence in this new job. I recommend you take it."

"Sir, with all due respect, this looks like a cover-up to save Farmingham's ass. She's worried the media will find out what happened and destroy her career. She doesn't give a rat's ass about those kids anymore. I can't forget about them. It's personal with me. I'm just a fucked-up detective, but I don't want any part of it."

"I respect you and what you've been through, so I'm going to pretend I didn't hear that insubordinate bullshit," Newman said. "Go away and clear your head for a while. I'm granting you personal leave for three months to recover from your injuries. If you haven't changed your mind by then, don't come back."

Ron's phone went dead.

Chapter Fifty-Nine

Ron was not the only one hurt in the blast. Mary Ann suffered a broken leg and a concussion. She took two weeks' medical leave and then hobbled back to work. Wilson suffered the worst injuries, a fractured skull along with a broken back. Luckily, there was no paralysis.

The three of them became instant heroes. Their pictures in the media made them highly recognizable around town, much to their annoyance. The brotherhood of police officers closed ranks and welcomed the detectives back into the hive. The Board of Supervisors awarded them medals of valor.

Wilson, because of his bad back, earned a cushy desk job when he returned to work, which he hated, along with a promotion to sergeant, which he liked. Mary Ann, already on the fast track, promoted to lieutenant.

At the press conference, Chief Newman stuck to the original story. "The detectives were there to arrest Art Garcia on suspicion of kidnapping Natalie Ramirez," he said. "We believe he blew himself up rather than surrender to authorities."

No one asked where he got the C-4 that caused the explosion.

The tabloids had other theories. They ran many stories, speculating that Garcia had terrorist ties. When cornered, he committed suicide with the bomb he planned to use against the White House, Los Angeles International Airport, the Santa Barbara County Board of Supervisors, or Disneyland. His sister was part of a sleeper cell, planning on creating more havoc before being killed to keep her quiet.

Forensics found no trace of Natalie Ramirez. The media speculated she was being held captive in the house and was torn apart by the explosion. The chief had no comment.

Only bits and pieces were found of Garcia, just enough to confirm identity through DNA analysis. By some miracle, his dog escaped nearly unscathed, after being thrown by the blast into the branches of a tree, where he was rescued by the fire department.

One month later, Roger Duncan announced his departure from Child Services to take a position in South Dakota. The Board of Supervisors lauded his years of excellent service to the county and wished him well. Behind the scenes, Farmingham gave him an ultimatum: quit or she would fire him. As he expected, he became the scapegoat.

Ricardo Rodriguez got reassigned as a "Special Assistant" to the Board, who gave him no responsibilities. He became the butt of many jokes, bitterly retiring from the County the following year, never understanding what he did to deserve such blacklisting.

Lieutenant Warner never got over being bypassed by the chain of command during the case. He retired a month later. The chief sent a flunky to present a plaque to him at his retirement party. Warner asked him to leave. The next day, the chief announced Mary Ann would be replacing him in charge of the police station.

Chief Newman, caught between fear of a media exposure by Ron, and Farmingham's desire to bury the case, decided not to run for reelection. "Now is the time to allow someone with fresh ideas to run for the office," he said. Taking his retirement pay, he moved with his wife to Idaho.

Later on that year, the Board of Supervisors announced a major project to create a new software program that would unite all the various county departments under one database. The Board touted the efficiencies this would create. Child Services and the Police Department would be the first to merge. This was the third time they announced this project, the media noted, and so far, the county had nothing to show for it.

The scandal of the eight missing children never became public knowledge. Notes on the case disappeared from the police files. Farmingham and Salido burned theirs. The rest of the Board of Supervisors was never told about the missing kids.

The murder investigation of Patsy Stonehead hit a dead end. There was no evidence she was killed by Art Garcia. Her case and Angela Garcia's remain unsolved.

Chapter Sixty

Ron sat motionless in a lawn chair in his backyard, watching a squirrel trying to climb up a steel pole he anchored in the ground to hold a bird feeder. The squirrel knew a tasty meal of seeds waited for him at the top. He had been there before. What he didn't know was that Ron greased the pole. It cracked him up to watch the rodent get halfway up only to lose traction and slide all the way to the bottom. *A metaphor for my whole life.*

It was late afternoon near the end of February. His backyard faced west. The warmth of the sun bathed his face as it slipped toward the ocean. It helped relax his facial muscles when a frequent headache bothered him.

Each day was almost the same as the last. He rarely ventured out unless he needed food. Most of the time he thought about the future, while healing from the headaches he still got occasionally. His personal leave would end in two more months, forcing a decision on whether he wanted to be a cop any longer. He already had the answer to that.

The ding dong of his doorbell interrupted his solitude. The sound panicked the squirrel, which gave up on the bird feeder and scampered away. Ron frowned but made no effort to rise. Instead, he closed his eyes and tilted his head back to catch the last rays of the sun, willing his headache to go away. A minute later, the gate to his backyard banged open, startling him. Mary Ann stood there, silhouetted in the opening. She looked pissed.

"You asshole. I've been leaving you messages for a month. Are you too busy working on your tan to reply? Is there a problem here I'm not aware of? Last I checked we are still partners, and a partner deserves some respect. So why don't you quit being a dick and talk to me?"

Ron gazed at her steadily and sighed. "Nice to see you, too. Heard you're the LT now. I expected to be getting a new partner."

Mary Ann opened her mouth to say something, but instead limped into the backyard and sat in a chair next to him. "Okay, let's get this straight. I'm not here in any official capacity. I'm here because we've got a history you and me. We both almost got killed, and I care about you. Something happened. Nobody will talk about it, but you got screwed somehow. Why else would you be here sitting on your ass for three months? So tell me what's going on. I was there with you, remember? I stuck my neck out there too."

"You were with me right up to the end, and then you bailed," he replied. "The chief gave you that promotion you always wanted, and you walked away from me. He bought your silence. So you're one of them now, and we've got nothing to talk about."

She sat back in her chair like he had slapped her. "The case was finished. All the suspects died. Nothing was left to walk away from. What happened between you and the chief?"

"You really want to get into that?"

"Yeah, I need to hear it."

Ron took a moment to collect his thoughts. "He offered me a staff job. Said the case was over. We did everything possible to solve it, but it was time to move on. I told him it looked to me like a cover-up by Farmingham, and he was going along with it. I turned the job down. Not going to be bought off."

"You mean the kids?" she said softly.

"Eight kids. How can we just let that go? I've got to find them, Mary Ann. Try to save them if I can. If we don't stop these guys, it's going to happen again and again."

She stood and started pacing. "What more could we have done? Everybody is dead. You're letting what happened with Becky affect your judgment."

He stiffened. "I've sat here and thought about this for a month. If I come back, I'm selling out these kids. No one will give a shit what happened to them. I lost my sister and yeah, it still hurts. It was my fault. Maybe if I find just one of these kids, it won't hurt so much. I'm going to resign from the force and start my own business as a private eye. Never going to give up looking."

"Are you crazy? You're only a couple of years away from a pension. Just cruise to the finish line in a staff job. Then you can do whatever you want."

He shook his head. "Work for Farmingham, knowing she gave me the job to buy my silence? I would rather be homeless in LA. Having this time to sit and think made me understand what was missing from my life—a purpose. Now I have one. My dad told me I could make a difference by becoming a cop. He didn't figure on people like Farmingham."

Ron was silent for a moment. "Follow your dreams. You might be the chief someday. But every time you see a little kid, you're going to think about this case."

Mary Ann's face flushed red. "You're wrong about

me. I care about those kids. I've got one too, remember? If any information surfaces in the future, I promise you I'm going to pursue it, regardless of the consequences. But I will not throw my whole career away to chase ghosts with you." She turned toward the gate. "Take care of yourself partner. My door is always open."

Ron watched her go as the last rays of the sun slipped into the ocean.

Epilogue

Article in the Santa Barbara Enquirer, January 10th
Mega-millions Jackpot Goes Unclaimed

The California State Lottery Commission announced today that the $135 million dollar lottery prize won last year on January seventh has gone unclaimed. Only one winning ticket had all the correct numbers. Per the lottery rules, the prize reverts to the state if it remains unclaimed for over a year. Lottery officials said the winning ticket came from the 7-Eleven convenience store on Paseo Grande Drive in Montecito.

A word about the author...

This is my first novel, and maybe the start of a third career. I hope you enjoyed it.

My life to this point has been spent in engineering and real estate appraising. I have a short story published and several others being reviewed. When not writing, I enjoy woodworking and walks with my dog.

CPSIA information can be obtained
at www.ICGtesting.com
Printed in the USA
LVHW012057101022
730380LV00013B/480